"I'll tell you what," Kit said, "you just give orders, and I will follow them."

"Speak for yourself," Shelby said.

"Would you rather take orders from me?"

She looked away from him quickly, and he realized that he'd stepped into something. Because she didn't fire anything right back at him, and he almost felt guilty about that.

And then she looked up at him, dark fire banked in her eyes. "I'd like to see you try."

He held back his answer. He held it back because everybody was here. He held it back because he didn't know how to make it not explicitly sexual.

He held it back, because the last thing in all the world he needed to do at this wedding preparation party was declare his sexual intent with his brother's future sister-in-law.

Especially when he knew that he couldn't have any intentions toward her at all.

* * *

Best Man Rancher by Maisey Yates
is part of The Carsons of Lone Rock series.

MAISEY YATES

BEST MAN RANCHER

HARLEQUIN®
DESIRE™

Recycling programs for this product may not exist in your area.

ISBN-13: 978-1-335-58138-9

Best Man Rancher

Copyright © 2022 by Maisey Yates

For questions and comments about the quality of this book, please contact us at CustomerService@Harlequin.com.

Harlequin Enterprises ULC
22 Adelaide St. West, 41st Floor
Toronto, Ontario M5H 4E3, Canada
www.Harlequin.com

Printed in U.S.A.

One

"Six inches is too long!" Shelby Sohappy glared across the table, across all the flowers piled on the table, across the tulle and the candy strewn over the table, to her older sister.

But it wasn't Juniper's reaction to Shelby's words that caught her attention, and held her there.

She felt it before she saw it. His response. *His*, always his. The change crackled through the air. And she told herself not to look. She told herself to keep her focus on Juniper, the bride, her sister, her best friend, and direct all wedding preparation complaints to her.

But she turned her head anyway.

As if he'd put his finger beneath her chin and

swiveled it toward him. That's how powerful the impulse to look was.

Kit Carson.

Damn Kit Carson.

Her eyes clashed with his, electric and upsetting. And his mouth curved—even more upsetting. "Six inches is too long? Maybe that's why I'm still single."

That earned a round of groans from the table— and Shelby should also groan. But instead she felt like her body had been lit up.

She had learned a lot since middle school.

That you didn't actually need algebra. That body glitter wasn't worth the hassle. That the girls who wouldn't let you sit with them would—in fact—peak once school ended and spend their adult years trying to reconnect with people they had once been mean to so that they could sell them lip gloss, leggings and the secrets of success and wealth and sisterhood, as long as you bought their weight loss shakes.

She'd learned that she was stronger than she'd imagined. That loss wouldn't kill you, even if you might wish it had.

But she hadn't learned how to control her physical response to Kit Carson, a man who was soon to be practically family, the best man to her maid of honor, her longtime, shame-fueled object of lust.

Yeah. She hadn't learned that.

"That's not why you're single, bro," said Chance, her sister's fiancé, and everyone laughed.

So Shelby laughed too. What choice did she have?

She felt like a foreign tourist pretending they understood what was happening around them. She was just lost. In ribbon curls and Kit Carson's excess of six inches.

How *many* inches more?

She didn't need to know the answer to that.

She didn't even need to *wonder* it.

Nope.

"Six inches," Juniper said, holding up a ribbon and a pair of scissors, and letting the edge glide effortlessly across it, resulting in a rather impressive curl, "is not too long at all."

Shelby ignored Chance and his brothers chuckling at that.

So did Juniper.

Shelby wondered, not for the first time, how the hell this had happened.

The Carsons and Sohappys had been enemies for generations. To the degree that the first time she'd spotted Kit Carson at a football game when she'd been in seventh grade and he'd been in tenth, she'd felt a deep, instinctive recoil in her soul.

At least, she liked to tell herself that's what it was.

Because it couldn't possibly have been anything else. She'd been dating Chuck already by then. Well, *dating* was a strong term. They'd been twelve, after all. They'd walked down to the diner in Lone Rock and had shared a milkshake with money Chuck had gotten collecting bottles and taking them to the can return.

They'd gone down to the river and skipped rocks.

They'd held hands. And he'd kissed her.

They'd started having sex when they were way too young, but hey, she'd been certain she'd marry him so the moral risk had seemed worth the reward.

And she'd been right.

She'd married Chuck pretty much as soon as high school had ended. She'd been so ready for that life. She'd loved him. Deep and uncomplicated.

And if she'd sometimes… If she'd been unable to keep herself from thinking of the man who'd first created a shiver of awareness inside her before she'd known what it was, she'd just blamed it on having been with only one man. Dismiss it as adventures she'd chosen not to have.

There had been moments in her marriage when she'd wondered if they'd done it too soon. If not dating other people had been a mistake.

When Chuck had died, she'd been so glad they'd had that life. That whole brilliant life.

From twelve to twenty-six. Thank God for all those years, because they hadn't gotten to grow old together. Just older.

She really didn't need to be thinking about any of this now.

But it was a wedding, so it was unavoidable.

And it was her sister's wedding, which made it more poignant.

Her sister's wedding to a Carson. That's what tipped it over into improbable.

"Who would have thought you'd be a bridezilla," Shelby groused.

Juniper was an EMT, and in general a very practical and nonsentimental soul. Before her engagement to Chance, anyway. Now suddenly it was all sentiment and fluffy dresses and ribbon curls.

"I haven't even begun to bridezilla," Juniper declared from her end of the table, which had all the Carson men looking worried.

The lone Carson girl—Callie, who had gotten married a while back and moved to Gold Valley, Oregon, a few hours away—was grinning. "I love this! I need more women in the family. To cause chaos and mayhem."

"You don't need any help with that, sis," Boone Carson said.

"I'm happy to contribute to family chaos!" Juniper said.

And Shelby couldn't help but feel just a little bit outside of all of this. It wasn't anyone's fault. Especially not Juniper's. Her sister deserved happiness. So much happiness. She had been there for Shelby in a profound way when Shelby had lost Chuck. And in all the time since. Juniper was her best friend.

But that didn't mean that Shelby couldn't find a way to have complicated feelings about this.

It made her think about her own wedding. And the terrible thing was… She didn't have a very clear memory of that day.

Which had seemed fine in the decade since it had occurred, when Chuck was still with her. She'd had the marriage. She hadn't needed more than good feelings and a few photos of the day.

She couldn't remember if they had sat around making wedding favors. She didn't think they had. Nobody should get married when they were eighteen. That was a whole fashion disaster. Shelby had worn a princess dress and a tiara. The entire thing had been a debacle. But of course, when you were eighteen, what you wanted out of the wedding was to be a princess. You thought a lot more about the wedding than you did the marriage. Not that her marriage hadn't been good. It had been. It had been great. Chuck had been her best friend, well, her other best friend, apart from her sister.

It was just, when you were eighteen you didn't really know what the rest of your life meant.

You still don't.

No. She didn't. Because her husband had gone and died and made her a widow in her midtwenties. But what the hell was she supposed to do with that?

Make ribbon curls, she supposed.

"We need to have all the wedding favors ready by tonight," Juniper said.

"Or heads will roll," said Chance, looking at Juniper as if seeking approval.

"That's right," Juniper said. "Heads will roll."

"Good luck with that," Shelby said.

"Yeah," Kit agreed, and she did her best to stop herself from looking at him, but much like her first best, this was not enough. Because she ended up looking at him. And he smiled. And she felt it. Hot and slow as it moved through her.

"If you make my bride upset," Chance said, looking right at his brother, "it'll be your head."

"If your bride can be upset about ribbon curl… I don't know, man."

"When was the last time you ever loved anything?" Chance said to his brother.

"I had a pretty damned good cheeseburger at about one o'clock today," Kit said. "I think I might've loved that."

She couldn't help it. She found herself laughing. And their eyes clashed again. This time, the electricity sent a shower of sparks through her, settling down between her thighs, and it made her twitchy.

This was the problem. When she had been in middle school, she had been able to write off the things that Kit Carson made her feel, but as she had hurtled toward adulthood, it had been impossible to pretend she didn't know.

But it was… It was wrong. It had been wrong because he was her enemy—by virtue of his family connection, nothing personal—and then it had been wrong—very wrong—because she was in love with another man.

Married to another man.

She gritted her teeth together. No. She wouldn't even think about it. She got up from the table, heading over to one of the coolers that were set around their little gathering. They had tables placed all around the yard, where different family members were helping with wedding favor assembly, and all around that were coolers with different beverages, and there was also a table full of snacks. She decided that it was definitely refreshment time.

She felt hot and unwieldy. Lost in the memories of the past, and the debate over ribbon curls, was the double entendre that had passed between herself and Kit. Well, not lost. It was just not the big thing that remained in the forefront. But the slow burn of it was left behind. She was uneasy, and she needed a moment with it.

She reached into the cooler and took out a bottle of beer. And then she heard footsteps, and straightened, looking across the cooler to see none other than Kit himself.

"Anything good in there?"

"They have the kind of beer that you would expect from a couple engaging in this level of wedding frippery. Does that answer your question?"

"Oddly, yes it does." He grinned, then reached

down into the cooler, and took out the first beer his hand closed around.

She felt like saying something sharp. She felt like being mean and making him walk away from her. But the truth of the matter was, all of this stuff… This stuff was one-sided. He didn't know that she had a long-standing hated attraction for him. And yes, they had clashed on a few occasions. So there was… There was a thing.

Though, she denied it. And had denied it on multiple occasions. In fact, she could remember clearly one time when they had been down at the Thirsty Mule, and he had been goading her, while offering to buy her and her friends a round of drinks—it had been girls' night out. And Kit had kept on making comments about how Shelby and he *didn't normally get along*. There was *a whole situation with her*, and she *didn't like him*. On and on. Until she had screamed at him at the top of her lungs: *you and I do not have a situation*.

Of course, for the rest of forever, everyone in town had convinced themselves that there was a situation.

Chuck had just laughed about it. Thankfully. And he had written off her umbrage as the normal sort of umbrage that her family felt whenever the Carson name was mentioned. And she had never had to admit that it wasn't just Kit's name that made her feel all out of sorts. It was the man himself.

He grabbed one of the bottle openers from the top

of the cooler and popped it easily. Then he reached out to grab her beer out of her hand. A few things happened simultaneously. The first was that his fingertips brushed hers. They were hot and rough, the way a man's hands were when he worked the land.

She didn't comprehend what was happening in the moment, and she did not release the hold on her beer.

Each of those realizations and moments occurred in one breath, and she found herself being dragged over the cooler into Kit.

"Easy," he said, taking hold of her arms. And she got an even more intense taste of the roughness of his hands. The heat there.

Oh, Lord. Oh, Lord, save her.

She was being tested, and she was failing. Here, at the preparation for her sister's wedding, she was having a full-blown attack of lust for a man who was about to be family-by-marriage. The man whom she had spent all these years pretending she had no situation with.

It was a situation.

"What the hell were you doing?" she asked, still clinging to her beer, still being held on to by him.

"I was gonna open your beer, Shelby," he said, peeling the bottle from her hands, while he set her back onto her feet. "Just a beer. Not a situation."

That bastard.

He had gone over that same night. Those same words.

It did something to her.

Meant something to her.

She wished it didn't.

"I didn't say that I needed help with the beer," she said.

He moved the edge of the bottle opener beneath the perforated cap and flipped it up. "No, you didn't. But I'm nice like that. A real gentleman, some might say."

"Who? Who has ever said that?"

"Not entirely sure."

"No one has ever said it."

He shrugged. "Someone must have."

"Not me."

"You're the president of my fan club. At least I thought so. If not, this is awkward. Because I thought…"

"You did not."

And she felt herself getting red, because… Because, all this banter was just a little bit too close to reality.

"We're not enemies anymore, or did you miss the memo."

"I missed *zero* memos. Believe me. And I tried to talk my sister out of this whole thing. You know, back when she lied to your brother about being her ranch hand when he had amnesia. And then fell in love with him. Yeah. I tried to interfere with all that."

"When you put it like that, it sounds vaguely ridiculous."

"It does," she said.

But ridiculous or not, it had occurred. That could honestly be the subtitle of a movie about her life. *Ridiculous or not, it had occurred.*

He lifted the beer bottle to his lips, and she couldn't help but watch the movement of his mouth, his throat working up and down as he took a long pull off the bottle. Why was he so damned compelling. Why? He didn't have any right to be. He was just a cowboy. They were a dime a dozen around here. Hell, he was one of six boys. There really was no call for him to be all this compelling. She had been married to a rancher. This one shouldn't stir...

She didn't want to think about this. She didn't want to be anywhere near Kit Carson while she was dealing with marriage and wedding feelings. She didn't want to think of him in a game of compare and contrast with Chuck and what she had felt for him.

She had loved Chuck. The love of her life. That phrase couldn't be truer about anyone or anything than it was about Chuck. She had loved him from the time she was twelve years old. And was certain that she would marry him from that same time. She had loved the man until the day he had died, and in all the days since. Kit Carson wasn't owed the same mental airspace as Chuck.

"You got your speech all nailed down?" he asked.

"Yes," she lied. "It's going to be the best speech."

"And you're ready for the bachelorette party?"

"More than ready."

They would be hosting the bachelor and bachelorette parties at the wedding venue. Which was going to be at a ranch about an hour away, up in the mountains, Green Springs Ranch. They were all going to stay in the different buildings on the property, and the wedding would take place in one of the main barns. As maid of honor, it was up to her to plan the bachelorette party. As best man, it was up to Kit to do the bachelor party.

"How did you end up being the best man, anyway?" she asked.

"I drew the short straw."

"What?"

"It's true. We never really figured on any of us getting married. Not us boys. I mean, there's Callie, but... Well, we didn't really figure on her getting married either. But she did. But you know, as far as the best man thing goes, we drew for it. I drew the short straw."

"Doesn't that imply that it's a bad thing?"

"I'm paying for the bachelor party. I'd say that's the short straw."

Suddenly, she felt boxed in. Observed by too many people, or maybe it was just him. The way that he always looked at her. Like he knew. But nobody could know. Nobody could ever know.

"Better go," she said. "The ribbons aren't going to curl themselves."

"Nope."

She turned away from him, and she ignored the way she could feel his gaze resting between her shoulder blades. Like a touch. A caress. Yeah. She ignored that because to acknowledge it would mean acknowledging the spark between them. And she absolutely refused to do that.

Two

Kit Carson wasn't an idiot. Despite reports to the contrary. In fact, he had a pretty damned good head on his shoulders. He might make dumbass decisions out riding the rodeo, bold and rash and dangerous when he flung himself on the back of an angry bull, determined to see him in an early grave, but that recklessness had netted him a damn good portfolio, personal wealth and a hell of a lot of prestige in the rodeo community.

Not to mention the attention of a great many buckle bunnies. And so, it was to his great and eternal mystery that Shelby Sohappy got underneath his skin to quite this degree.

And it wasn't recent. The woman *always* had.

Dating someone else, engaged. *Married.* He had felt drawn to her like a moth to a flame. Like a deer in headlights. Like some other cliché he couldn't think of right now. All he knew was that he really wanted to see her naked.

He could have his pick of women. He had. But there was something about her. About the way they sparked heat off each other, the way that he flustered her, that made him interested. But she was off-limits. She'd been off-limits for a long time, but in all honesty, he figured another man's marriage was that man's responsibility. He had never made a move on Shelby, but he figured whether or not her marriage put her off-limits was up to her. Now that the Carsons and the Sohappys were no longer enemies, well, that changed things a fair bit. Now she was going to be essentially family. And that meant there could be absolutely no… Nothing. Anything.

Because that would make things difficult for Chance. And Kit didn't want to make things difficult for Chance. They had had a difficult enough life as it was.

Chance had found love, and good for him. Kit didn't have it in him.

Losing their sister Sophie when they were kids had just been too much for him. The loss, the feeling of failure when all the caregiving he did couldn't save her…

He'd been twelve and that weight had never shifted.

And more than that, the ongoing grief in the family.

He loved his mom, his dad, his brothers and his youngest sister, Callie, so damned much. And losing Sophie to a terminal illness had underlined how dangerous that love was.

Then there was Buck, his oldest brother, who'd been involved in a horrible car accident that had left him scarred, distant from everyone. They hadn't seen him in years and there was nothing Kit had been able to do to fix it.

There was just so much pain to manage in his family.

Lord.

He didn't want more of it. He never wanted a wife or kids. He didn't even want a dog. He didn't want to love any new thing.

That was the thing. He didn't love Shelby Sohappy. He wasn't even really sure if he liked her. He just wanted her. He was a man who knew that chemistry superseded common sense pretty much any day of the week. He had accepted that what they had was some kind of superior chemistry. The kind you couldn't manufacture even if you wanted to. And you wouldn't want to, but if you could, you would definitely direct it at somebody you'd never see again. Or someone who wouldn't get tangled up in your life. At least, that was what was ideal to *him*.

So yeah. Nothing much had changed. He couldn't have her back when she'd been married. He couldn't have her now. There had been a very small window where he might've been able to have her, but she'd been grieving. Fair enough.

He knew about grief. He knew how it changed you. How it fucked you up big-time. Changed the way that you saw the world. Broke down all the landscape inside you and didn't bother to rebuild the damn thing.

Yeah. He knew about grief. And it was knowing about that kind of grief that made him all the more determined to stay the hell away from this woman.

Too bad they were going to be in proximity for the planning of this wedding. They wouldn't be most of the time. He assumed that for holidays Chance and Juniper would go back and forth between the families, and Shelby didn't have anything to do with the Carsons specifically. But just for right now the woman was squaring his path.

He did his best not to think about how soft her golden brown skin had been beneath his fingers when he held her there. Dammit she was beautiful. Her thick black hair was cut into a chin-length style that highlighted the heart shape of her face, her high cheekbones, her deep brown eyes. Her lips were full and dusky, a caramel color that he wanted to lick.

And he needed to not think of that. Not right now. "There's dessert."

He looked across at the table where all the food was, and saw his mother setting three giant cheesecakes covered with caramel down onto the tabletops.

Dammit all. Caramel. That was really what he wanted to think about right now. In context.

Everybody made a grateful noise and he gathered around the table along with all of them, getting his piece and returning with it to the assembly point.

"The wedding is in just three days," Juniper said, as if they needed reminding. "And we need to get everything up to the venue and get it all set up."

"I don't know why the hell you didn't just get married at the Carson ranch," Kit said.

Juniper gave him a scathing look. "I'm not letting you win like that."

"Getting to host the wedding would be winning?"

Chance held up a hand. "Believe me. I have had that conversation. Back out now. You won't win."

"Now that's what I like," Juniper said. "A Carson admitting when he's beaten."

"It's just a Carson admitting he knows how to choose his battles," Chance said, grunting.

"Well, it's no problem," Kit said. "There's no shortage of pickup trucks between us. We can carry whatever the hell you need up that way."

"I got a pickup truck too," Shelby said. "And I'm the maid of honor."

"I don't think we need all the pickup trucks we have between us," Juniper said.

His eyes met Shelby's again, and she looked away, faint color on her cheekbones. She felt it too. He knew she did. He'd always known that. What he didn't know was what story exactly she told herself.

It didn't matter. He might want Shelby, but there was no way in hell he would ever do anything to make her his. She was the marriage-and-family type. She'd been in love, and she lost that love. He didn't want to step into that. Not even a little.

"I'll tell you what," Kit said. "You just give orders, and I will follow them."

"Speak for yourself," Shelby said.

"Would you rather take orders from me?"

She looked away from him quickly, and he realized that he…stepped into something. Because she didn't fire anything right back at him, and he almost felt guilty about that.

And then she looked up at him, dark fire banked in her eyes. "I'd like to see you try that."

He held back his answer. He held it back because everybody was here. He held it back because he didn't know how to make it not explicitly sexual.

He held it back, because the last thing in all the world he needed to do at this wedding preparation party was declare his sexual intent with a woman he was inextricably linked to through his brother's relationship with her sister.

Especially when he knew that he couldn't have any intentions toward her at all.

Shelby was exhausted, carrying all the baskets of various things into her cabin.

Juniper was helping, basket after basket of different wedding favors coming in after the other.

"You know," Shelby said, "I'm trying not to be nosy, or in your business, but aren't you marrying a superrich cowboy?"

Juniper laughed. "What's your point?"

"My point is, you had to make all of this. The guy could *buy it*. Why are we doing favors for every table, and ribbon curls?"

Juniper looked at her, confusion etched into her features. "You really don't know?"

"I mean, your pride, I assume."

She shook her head. "I don't have any of that with Chance. We're getting married. We have a partnership. We don't divide things up, and we certainly don't keep score on what's his and what's mine or any of that. It isn't that. It's just I wanted to do this because this is what we did for your wedding."

Shelby blinked. "Is it? I was just trying to remember. And I couldn't. I just remembered the wedding dress. Which, by the way, you should've talked me out of."

"I loved it."

"Well. You were also a teenage girl. Neither of us were trustworthy."

"Do you really not remember? We wrapped all those different terra-cotta pots that we found for cheap down at the dollar store in pretty paper, made paper ribbons, and you had those potted plants up all around in the wedding venue."

She frowned, her forehead creasing. "Yeah. I do remember that. It's weird. I just don't… I don't think about it much."

"I'm sorry. I didn't mean to bring up a painful memory."

"I've been thinking about Chuck all day." Truth be told, she thought about him most days. "It's unavoidable."

Juniper looked worried. "You didn't say anything about it."

"I don't want to make your wedding about my issues. It isn't about my issues. Your wedding is about you. And I'm so happy for you."

"You seem like you maybe aren't sometimes."

"It's not that. I think it's a little bit strange that you're marrying a Carson. All things considered. But I'm coming to terms of it."

"And it has nothing to do with Kit?"

She narrowed her eyes. "Don't push it." Juniper had never mentioned Kit, or Shelby's non-situation with Kit, until recently. Shelby didn't like the new development.

"Did something happen between you two?"

"No! When would anything have ever happened?"

"I don't know. I've never known. All I know is that when you see him…"

"Please don't finish that sentence, because my pride is hanging on by a thread, because I nearly fell down into the man tonight, and I don't need anything to compromise what remains of it. It is tenuous. At best."

"I don't think anyone else can tell," Juniper said quickly. "It's just that I know you. I know you really well."

"And you know me well enough to know that if I don't want to talk about it I'm not going to talk about it."

Juniper nodded, "You're right. I do know you well enough to know that. Sorry."

"It's fine. Like I said. I'm a little bit surprised, both because of his family, and the circumstances…"

"Oh, the thing that I did that you absolutely disapproved of because it was really messed up?"

"Yeah. That thing. Where you lied to the guy about who you were? And who he was?"

"It worked out," Juniper said. She winced. "Believe me. I have apologized many times over. And I do feel bad about it. Though, forgetting who he was… And me treating him like he was somebody different… It was the only way that we could really get to know each other. I know it sounds imbalanced. But… It's just how it works."

Shelby couldn't help it. Right in that moment, she sort of wished that she could have that. A moment to be somebody new. Maybe she needed to leave town. She had never really considered it before.

Losing Chuck had been destabilizing in every way. Leaving Lone Rock, leaving their land…leaving her parents, her grandparents—that was something that she couldn't even fathom. But it was hard to be here. Hard to be in a place where everybody knew who you were, where everybody knew your life story. So they looked at you like you were sad even when you had never exchanged three words with them, because they already knew through the grapevine exactly what you'd been through.

"I can see how that would work," she said, her voice feeling scratchy.

"It did work," Juniper said. "So are you going to head up to the venue early?"

Shelby looked around at all the things. "I don't see how it will work if I don't. I need to get everything set up for the bachelorette party, and I need to get all the party favors up there for that. Plus the wedding."

"He has six brothers. He will absolutely handle whatever needs handling."

"I'm your only sister," she said, fiercely. "And it means more to me now than it ever has. Your… You and Mom and Dad and Grandma and Grandpa are all I have. I was supposed to make a family, an expanded family with Chuck. And I… I want to do everything for you. Just trust me."

Juniper looked at her, her dark eyes steady and level, and filled with compassion, and it put Shelby back to that night three years ago when Juniper had come over to tell her…

When Juniper'd had to be the one to tell her Chuck was in a car accident, and he hadn't made it.

Her sister was real. Genuine. When she said she wanted to be there for Shelby, it wasn't an empty gesture. She'd proved it that night. She hadn't passed the job off on someone else. She'd been the one to do it. She'd been the one to hold Shelby while she'd cried like she'd never stop.

"Oh, Shelby," Juniper said. "I'm so sorry that this is hard."

She loved that Juniper cared so much, but she really didn't want to take the focus off her either. This was her moment. Her love story.

Shelby was happy for her.

"I don't want this to be about me. I really don't. This is about you and your happiness. And I am thrilled for you. Yeah, weddings make me think about my own wedding. But don't think for one second that you're causing me any sadness. You couldn't. I live with the loss. Every day. He was part of my life for so long, and then just one day having him gone completely… It's awful. But it's different than it was right at first. And it isn't… I don't know how to explain this in a way that makes sense, but it isn't your wedding making me sad. It's making me think about my wedding. But that isn't thinking about him more than usual."

"Thanks. I love you."

"I love you too."

They hugged, and Juniper left. Left Shelby with all these baskets.

Yeah. She was going to have to get them up to the venue, but actually, maybe that would be a good thing. It would give her a little bit of time to herself. A little bit of time to reflect.

The thing that made her feel guilty, really guilty, was that sometimes she was just tired of grieving. Just tired of… Of living with loss. She wanted to be done with it. But that was hardly fair. Chuck couldn't really stop being dead.

She laughed. She needed to move his things out of their bedroom. His clothes. She had gotten some out when Juniper had borrowed them for Chance. She hadn't taken them back. Hadn't put them back in the closet when they'd been returned to her. It had felt like a baby step. An important one.

But this house that she lived in alone still had the hallmarks of a home that was shared. And at some point she was going to have to change that.

There were other things that probably needed to change. She should make a crafting room out of that spare bedroom. Even though she didn't craft. She should make it a reading nook. Because it was never going to be what she had dreamed of it being. Even with Chuck, they hadn't been able to turn that spare room into a nursery.

There was no way that was going to change.

But letting go was just so hard. And sometimes… Shelby didn't understand why she had to be the one to let go of so many things.

But her sister was getting married. And they were going to have a bachelorette party. One of epic proportions.

If Juniper wanted to hearken back to Shelby's wedding… Well, Shelby owed her a little bit of revenge, actually.

She smiled.

Oh yes. The bachelorette party was going to be an epic night to remember.

Three

Kit, Jace, Flint and Boone were all down at the Thirsty Mule getting drinks. The ramshackle old saloon had been the heart of Lone Rock since the late 1800s. It had the original saloon doors still swinging between the entryway and the bar. It was rumored the hole up at the top had come from a bullet that had shot the piano player stone-cold dead back in 1899.

Kit had it on good authority that it was actually from a jackass who put a pool cue through it in 1980.

Jace's best friend, Cara, was serving beers gamely from behind the bar, and Kit would be remiss if he passed up the chance to make a sly comment about his brother's friend in his presence. "Cara is looking pretty good."

Jace didn't look at him. "I will kill you. With my bare hands. And I'll enjoy it."

Jace insisted he was only friends with Cara. Kit believed him, mostly. Jace was also very protective of Cara, so whatever the reason, Kit's commenting on Cara's beauty often caused chaos. And Kit lived for it.

He grinned. "Why don't you just marry her already?"

"What are you, eight?" Jace asked.

"No. I am not eight. If I were eight I would be suggesting you marry the beer because you love it."

"I hate you."

"Hey," said Flint. "We are here to discuss our brother's bachelor party."

"Right, right. I'm the best man," said Kit, "so this is primarily my responsibility."

"Strippers," said Boone.

"Hell no," said Jace.

"I'm sorry, why are you opposed to exotic dancers?" Kit asked.

"Since this is the kind of event people are going to hear about." He tilted his head toward Cara.

"Again," Kit said, "if you are so beholden to Cara and what she thinks, you might as well marry her."

Cara began to walk toward them then, her blond hair pulled back in a ponytail, a short, spiked leather jacket making the point of her general demeanor for her. "What's that, Kit?"

"I said," Kit responded, grinning, "if Jace is going to be whipped by you, he might as well marry you."

"I won't marry him," said Cara. "I can't be tamed."

"I'd be happy to tame you for a while," Kit said, which earned him a glowing smile from Cara. All in with the intent of pissing Jace off.

"I will kill you," said Jace.

"Jace," said Cara. "Please. If anyone is going to kill Kit it'll be me. Or Shelby Sohappy."

The mention of Shelby's name was like a fire-cracker going off in his gut. "She doesn't have it in her."

"Yes, she does," said Boone. "She would kill you with a smile on her face. And she's got enough land that they'd never find your body."

Boone was a terminal smart-ass. He and his best friend in the rodeo, Daniel, had a reputation for being hell-raisers. Though Daniel was married and had set-tled in theory, rumor had it he hadn't changed at all.

He often wondered what Boone thought about his friend's behavior. It was tough to tell what Boone thought about anything.

Too much of a smart-ass, that was the thing.

"Well, good thing she has no reason for wanting to kill me."

"That's not really what I've observed," said Cara.

"Ah, right. I forgot. The all-seeing, all-knowing bartender," Kit said.

"You guys have a thing."

"We do not have a thing," Kit said. "In fact, she once told me that we have no situation at all."

"You don't say that to someone you don't have a thing with," Cara said. "If there's no situation, there's no need to remark upon the situation."

Kit shrugged. The fact was, they did have a thing, and he knew it. That *thing* was chemistry. But Kit liked his chemistry with women the way he liked his chemistry classes. Over quickly. Handled. Done. Graduated from. He was a satisfy-them—multiple times—and-leave-them type. He had done serious way early on in his life. He knew what it was like to have the burden of taking care of someone, and he never wanted it again. He had a huge family, and he loved them. All of them. Even Buck, who was gone. It was exhausting. He didn't need to love anyone else. Not ever.

"Whatever you say, Kit. But anyway, why are you assuming that Jace is beholden to me? He can do whatever he wants."

"He wants to hire strippers for the bachelor party."

Cara looked at him, her eyes like daggers. "I'll never speak to you again, Jace Carson."

"Just a second," said Kit, peering behind Cara at some of the jars at the back shelf of the bar.

"What are you doing?"

"Checking to see if you have Jace's balls back there."

Cara was unmoved. She planted her hands squarely on the bar and leaned toward him, staring.

"And what are you doing, Cara?" he asked.

"Checking to see if you got any human decency in there. Because Jace has it. He is almost a gentleman."

Boone laughed so hard he nearly fell off the bar stool. "Jace Carson. A gentleman. That's because you only see him here in Lone Rock. And you never see him on the road. You've only seen a piece of him, sweetheart."

"Call me sweetheart one more time and you can find out whether or not the spikes on this jacket are a decoration or for practical purposes."

"That's my girl," said Jace.

She walked away from them, and Kit was just mad that she had managed to redirect his thoughts right back to Shelby.

Right. Like they were ever all that far from her to begin with.

That was the problem with Shelby. She was under his skin, and he couldn't even really say why. Just sex. That was the thing. He wanted her, and he had never been able to have her. Maybe he wanted her in part because she was so… So decidedly off-limits. Actually, it should be a little bit more resolvable these days. She was single, and the barrier had been broken between their families. Juniper and Chance were already getting married. There was nothing forbidden about an association between the two of them at all.

That should make her less interesting. That should make him entirely less aroused by the thought of grabbing her and pulling her up against his body, lowering his head and tasting whether or not her lips were sugary, salty caramel like he imagined…

Dammit.

"So, what is the bachelor party plan, then?" Boone asked.

"Well, because I don't want our mother to kill us, I was never planning on hiring any strippers. However, I was thinking skeet shooting, some drinking. Darts. Pool. There's kind of a bachelor pad house up there, all outfitted for this kind of thing. And, we need to have a camping trip."

"A camping trip?" Boone questioned.

"Yeah. Like we did when we were kids."

They didn't talk about why. It was just one of those things. But the boys had gotten sent out of the house quite a bit when their sister Sophie had been sick and recovering from different treatments. Having the campout in the backyard was a way to get the house quiet for her.

It wasn't a bad memory. Not really. But that time would always be bittersweet.

It was something that they shared. All of them.

"All right."

"Yeah, I figured it would be good. Hell, we didn't get to send Callie out into the world with any warning. She just went and eloped."

"Yeah. With Jake Daniels. Of all the things."

"She seemed happy enough."

She was taken care of. And that was a big load off Kit's mind. When she had first come back to the ranch with him, Kit had been… Not very happy. He knew Jake from the rodeo circuit, and as far as he was concerned, Jake was a bad bet. He had been the kind of guy who was… Well, he was like all of them. He was a ho. A shameless, uninhibited man ho. And, the idea of him marrying Kit's sister had gone down like a lead balloon. But he had proved to Kit that he loved Callie. And more than that, he had proved that he was committed to Callie's safety. And that mattered. It mattered a whole hell of a lot. Because he had spent all of Callie's childhood worrying about her safety, and then she had gone and gotten the rodeo bug. And she couldn't do something sane like riding barrel horses. No. His sister had gone and gotten the bug to ride saddle bronc. And she had been insistent about it. Their dad had done basically everything in his power to block her from doing it, but she had gotten around that by marrying Jake and getting access to her trust fund.

But, the thing was, she was great at it.

She was great at riding saddle bronc. And she really brought something fresh and new to the event. She had invigorated rodeo-goers. And he had to be proud of her. From a feminist perspective even. But as an older brother, not so much. And there were just two different kinds of things that existed inside him. He was all for equality. But a lot less so when it came to the health and safety of his little sister. Let somebody else blaze trails. Blazing trails was dangerous, and he had a hard time admitting that it was all right for Callie to be out there doing it.

But Jake cared about her safety so much that it gave Kit some room to breathe.

"I'm planning to go up to the wedding ranch and check things out tomorrow," Kit said. "Get some supplies delivered, get the house opened up and set to go."

"I've got a date," said Boone. "So, I won't be up till a little later."

"You have a date," Kit said. "With who?"

"You know, I don't remember her name. But, she's one of the rodeo queens. She's coming through town, and I'm not gonna miss it."

"Great. Enjoy your booty call."

"I promised Cara I'd help her with a few things. But I'll be there the day before the wedding."

"You better the hell be. That's when the party's happening."

"Great. Well. We'll see you out there in a couple of days," said Flint.

"Yeah. Assholes. See you in a couple of days."

Shelby had somehow managed to get all the baskets of favors into the back of her truck, and all of the favors for the bachelorette party into the back

seat. She was feeling pretty good about everything.
She had some great favors for the bachelorette party,
and she had been mean.

Because Juniper had been mean to her.

The problem with having your equally young and
immature sister plan your bachelorette party when
you were getting married at eighteen was that *everything* was immature.

Penis everything.

And so, Shelby had retaliated. Meanly. And with
grown-ass adult money and the full power of the in-
ternet, that meant she'd been able to take what Juniper had accomplished and turn it up to the tenth
power.

And she didn't care if her sister liked it or not.

Now, there would be real decorations too, but
she'd had to get penis straws, a penis crown and,
best of all, a very large vibrator to be the center-
piece of some flowers. She figured that Juniper and
Chance might appreciate the gift.

They could take it on their honeymoon.

For just a moment, that stopped her short. She
really didn't want to think about her sister hooking
up and having sex. But the subject of honeymoons,
and the thought of the vibrator, brought it all close
to mind.

You don't need the guy. Just the vibrator.

And she had her own, thank you very much. She

had invested in a pretty decent collection of them during this stretch of single time.

Eventually… Eventually there would have to be a guy. Wouldn't there? Eventually there would have to be one just so she didn't go crazy.

Except, she couldn't imagine it. Couldn't imagine being with anybody except for…

Unbidden, an image of Kit popped into her mind. No. She had spent way too many years being disciplined about him. She had never fantasized about him, no matter how it had hovered around the edges of her consciousness. Not while she was with Chuck, and not since. She was not going to undo all that good moral fiber in a moment of weird weakness.

So she shut that out of her mind. She was fine. And she wasn't envious. If she wanted to hook up, she could go hook up. It wasn't even flattering. Men were disgusting. They would literally hump a tree if given half the chance. It wasn't like she wouldn't be able to find somebody. There was nothing wrong with her.

She stood there in the driveway of the farmhouse where they would be having their girls' night. And she felt like that thought fell a little bit flat. It wasn't like there was anything wrong with her.

There was something sad in her.

Something a little bit dampened.

Broken.

Something that wondered if it would ever feel *alive* again.

Yeah, the thing about grief was, it changed. It didn't go away.

But there was a hole in your life where someone had once been, and the passage of time didn't make it stop being there. It didn't make that person not gone. For a while there, the grief had gotten worse.

Because it had been even longer since she'd seen Chuck. As silly as that sounded. For a few months it had been like… Maybe he was on a trip. Maybe he would come back. But at six months… She remembered very distinctly realizing she had not been away from Chuck for that long ever. Not since she had met him. It wasn't a vacation amount of time. It was significant. And it left her feeling raw and hollow.

That had gone away. That part of it. There were all those firsts she had to get through.

And there is a first you haven't gotten through yet.

She just didn't want to. Not yet.

She had kind of underestimated how her sister's being in a relationship would bring a bunch of stuff up to the surface for her, and she didn't want it to poison this experience. She wanted her sister to have this. Wanted her sister to have a good time. Wanted it to be all about her. Wanted it to be special.

She did not want it to be about her pain. She just… She couldn't bear her own pain. She was sick of herself.

So she focused on her immaturity, her amusement at it all. And started taking trips from the house to the car.

The ranch was beautiful, set high atop a mountain overlooking the valley below. It had a gorgeous little farmhouse, a huge barn where they held all of the events, very rustic, and different from the one on Carson land, which was a bit too slick, according to Juniper.

There was another house spaced out in a different part of the property that Juniper had mentioned the men would be staying in.

The men.

Well, they weren't here right now. Shelby was by herself.

As if that's remarkably different from every other day?

No. She supposed it wasn't. But at least she wasn't alone in her house. It was a different kind of alone. It almost felt like a vacation.

She saved the load of penises for last. And she did laugh, when she pulled the big laundry basket that contained all those party favors out, and began to cart them toward the house.

"Well, fancy meeting you here."

She turned around, her eyes wide, and jostled the basket, one phallic straw springing out and down to the ground below.

Great.

Her basket of cocks overfloweth. In front of Kit.

"What are you doing here, Kit?"

"Same thing as you, I imagine." And then, he seemed to realize what was in the basket she was holding. "Well, no. Not the same thing as you."

"Did you not have a basket of dick paraphernalia for the bachelor party?"

"Suddenly I feel remiss," he said.

She was doing her level best to cling to what little dignity she had and it was tough. It was real tough.

"It's not too late," she said.

"Do you have an extra?"

"Do I have an extra… Penis?"

A smile spread, slow and dirty over his face, and she wanted to… Punch him. She really wanted to punch him. "I just have the one, that's all."

She felt like she was going to choke. On horror, heat, arousal, or maybe all three. "Wow. Well, this has been delightful. How long are you up here for?"

"Until the wedding."

"You're not serious," she said.

"I am serious. I'm here to the wedding because there are some things to set up."

"No," she said. "No, because… I'm here until the wedding."

"Is that a problem?"

"No," she said.

"Good."

"Like I told you. We don't have…"

"We don't have a situation," he said, his eyes giving off way too much heat.

"Not even a little one. Not at all."

"Good to know. I'm glad. Because I want the wedding to be perfect. And I would hate for anything to interfere."

"Nothing will interfere."

"Good. In fact, we could probably be of some use to each other. What do you think?"

She blinked. And really, she had no reason to refuse him. If there were things that could be done, things that they could do collaboratively… It actually just made sense. Because the truth of the matter was, nothing had ever happened between them. Nothing beyond a few warmish exchanges that had left her feeling flustered. And that was all her. Kit was Kit, which meant that he was a flirt, because he didn't know another way to be. It was simply how he was, and that was the way of it. She knew that. There was no reason to go getting heated up.

So yeah. Why not. But not now. Because right now was awkward.

"Well. I'm just going to… Take my basket of penises and go."

"Okay."

"Maybe I'll have a bath."

"Okay."

And suddenly she felt overly hot, because it was

like her mouth was just saying things, and she didn't have any control over it.

"I'm out of practice," she said. "With the talking to people. That I'm not related to. Sorry."

He nodded slowly, and right then, his expression did something sort of genuine. "I'm sorry," he said. "I'm sorry about your husband."

That he linked her lack of social skills with her loss was…weirdly touching. His awareness of it, of her as a person, was sort of unexpected. She didn't know what to do with it.

"Thank you."

She swallowed hard, and went into the house, and just as she did, she remembered what Juniper had told her about their family. That they'd had a sister. And she died when they were kids.

That was why he looked at her like that. That was why he said it with that kind of gravity. It was why he knew *I'm sorry* was enough. Because there were no platitudes that made it okay. There was no grand speech to give that was going to magically make it all less painful. It just… Was. It was lost. The loss was lost. You couldn't fix it. Couldn't go back. Couldn't change it. Couldn't hold on to him for five more minutes before he walked out the door to change the timing so that when the other pickup truck crossed the yellow line his car wasn't there. No. She couldn't go back. She couldn't fix it. She wasn't prescient. She hadn't been able to prevent it. She hadn't even had a bad feeling about the day.

No. She'd been over it a hundred times. Magical thinking didn't have any kind of place in the grief sphere.

And the way he'd said that. All practical. He knew. He knew. And she really appreciated that.

Who would've thought that she would appreciate an encounter with Kit. Well. And who would've thought that she would be standing in front of him with a basket full of phalli. But, it was that kind of day. It was just that kind of day.

And she really was going to take a long hot bath and put all of it out of her mind.

Four

The bachelor house was a big log cabin filled with animal heads and cowhide everywhere. He loved it. This was the kind of place where he would like to settle down. They all had cabins on their parents' property, and there really was no reason to buy up, especially when he was still traveling with the rodeo during the season. But the places at his parents' house were slick. They weren't this country. And he really liked things being this country.

He paused at the doorway and looked across the expanse of fields. It was dark now. But he could see a light on in the window of the farmhouse just across the way.

Shelby Sohappy.

They were on the same mountain. And there was nobody else around. That really was something. And he needed to stop thinking of her that way. It was difficult, considering she had been standing there with a whole barrel of sex toys.

He did not need to think about Shelby and sex toys. Not in the same sentence. Not in the same... Oh, the same fantasy. And it was getting there. It was getting there quick.

This was the problem with small towns. It was like they'd been engaging in foreplay for years on end. But he really was sorry about her husband. He tried to focus on that. He had liked Shelby's husband. He'd been a nice guy. He used to run into him out on occasion. He'd sometimes even sit with the Carsons and have a beer. He had just always told them never to tell his wife, considering the family had such a rivalry. But, being outside of the family, he hadn't internalized it to the degree that Shelby and Juniper did.

Yeah. He had been an easygoing guy. Short and stocky with dark hair and an easy smile. It really was a shame. A tragedy.

Too bad Kit had always wanted the guy's wife.

Didn't make it not a tragedy in the abstract, though.

It was one of the things that Kit would never understand about the world. The way that the good seemed to die young and terribly. And leave voids in the world that nobody could ever fix.

It was why he preferred to have as few connections as possible.

Well, *preferred* wasn't even a strong enough word. He lived his life by that code. By that creed. He hadn't fully appreciated the connections that would end up being built, though, when his siblings started to get married. He just had so many damn siblings. Callie had gotten married, and Jake Daniels had been brought into the fold. If they ever had kids, there would be nieces and nephews. And then there was Chance and Juniper. And the same went for them.

Babies.

Babies freaked him out.

They were so soft and vulnerable. When Callie had been little, he didn't think he'd ever gotten a wink of sleep. That was the problem with being a kid who'd watched his sister die.

You didn't trust anything. That was just it. He didn't trust anything, so it was better to just not love much.

He hadn't had any choice when it came to his family. They were big and boisterous. And he loved them with everything he had.

But he didn't have to add more people to the list.

While he was looking out across the way, the lights turned off. And he would've thought nothing of it, except there were lights on on multiple floors and in multiple windows, and they all went out simultaneously. So unless there was some kind of smart-switch situation happening—and out here he seriously doubted it—he had reason to feel a little bit concerned.

He hustled out the front door without thinking, and jogged across the field, heading toward the farmhouse. And just as he was about to knock on the door, it opened up.

"Oh," she said.

"Hey," he said. "What happened?"

"The lights went out," she said, her cheeks illuminated.

"Oh. Well. I can come in and take a look if you like. I got a flashlight out in the truck."

"Thanks, I…"

"Alternatively, you could come stay in the bachelor pad."

"Oh," she said. "No."

She didn't like this. His pushing her. But she needed help, and he didn't see why he shouldn't offer it. He didn't see why there needed to be such a big wall built between the two of them. Not now anyway.

"There's like ten rooms in there. And they're all vacant. And then, in the morning, we can sort out whatever the hell happened here. Seems better than stumbling around in the dark."

"Yeah, I guess so."

"Go get your suitcase."

"It's just an overnight bag."

She disappeared, then came back a moment later. She looked… She looked afraid. At least, as far as he could tell with only her cell phone flashlight lit up.

"You don't *have* to come with me. I can try to figure out why the lights went out here."

"No," she said. "No. You don't have to do that. It's fine. Let's just go. I'm starving. And with the lights out I can't cook any food and…"

"Do you have stuff in the fridge?" he asked.

"I have it in a cooler."

"I brought some steak. And I do have power. So I'm happy to grill for us both."

"I don't want to eat your steak," she said, wrinkling her nose.

"Hey. You offered to lend me a penis. So… I feel like it's a fair trade."

She choked, and tried to cover it with a cough. "Well, I didn't bring any of them with me."

"I'll take a rain check."

"That's very reasonable of you," she said, still wheezing.

"I'm very reasonable."

He reached out and took the overnight bag from her hands. But this time, he was careful not to touch her. When he had tried to help with the beer, he had touched her. And it had set off a whole thing.

He didn't need to go setting off whole things. Not again.

So they walked across the field together in relative silence, toward the bachelor pad.

And when they walked up the front porch and inside, she made a scoffing noise. "Well. I can see why they were putting you all up in here."

"Yeah. Who was all staying in your place?"

"Your sister. My mother. A couple of friends from high school. But this is going to be…"

"Oh yeah. There's a lot of us. And it's a lot of testosterone."

"Sounds great."

"I don't really think you mean that."

"Well, since you're offering to cook me steak, I'm actually not going to push you."

She hung back, though in the doorway, as he went inside.

He went into the kitchen, and got the steaks out of the fridge. They were sitting in a marinade, because he wasn't an animal. The thing about being a bachelor was if you were committed to that kind of lifestyle, then you needed to learn how to take care of yourself. And Kit liked good food.

He didn't see the point in living like a trash animal just because in many ways he philosophically was one.

"I'm grilling anyway," he said. "I had it preheating outside."

"Wow. I feel kind of honored."

A strange, haunted look crossed over her face. He

had a feeling she was thinking about another time. Another man.

And that is why you don't want to get involved.

"Yeah. You like… Grilling?"

"Obviously I don't," she said.

Dammit. He had been trying to ask an innocuous question, and he'd gone and stepped right into it.

"Yeah. No. I mean…"

"Yes. My husband used to grill."

He was still here, that guy, even though he wasn't here. Kit knew how that worked. He felt bad that he'd missed a connection here, with her. That he hadn't been more careful.

"Right. Sorry."

"You don't have to say *sorry*. It's… I mean, it's not as painful now. I just think about it all the time. You know, because you realize how absurd it is you can't turn and say something to someone who used to always be there. But they'll never be there again. It's ridiculous. So how can you… Not think about it?"

"Yeah. I know."

She nodded gravely. And he had a feeling she really did know that he knew. So that was good. He didn't have to explain it. He was not looking to have a heart-to-heart with her. Nothing that was personal. He wasn't looking to have a heart-to-heart with anybody.

"Grill's back here," he said, pushing open the double doors that led out to the grand outdoor kitchen area. It was a lot spiffier out there than it was inside.

"Wow," she said, looking up. It made him look up too. The stars above were a brilliant blanket of diamonds, and he really figured he didn't take enough time to appreciate that sort of thing. But he just didn't think much about it. Miracles and wonders and all that kind of stuff had been rendered pretty moot for him back when Sophie had died.

He had hoped.

That was the thing. Because he thought that the good guy won. And there was nobody better than his beautiful, tough little sister. And then it was like the safety net in everything had been pulled away. It hadn't made them afraid. Because Sophie hadn't done anything risky to get sick. He'd figured if death was out there... Well, then it would come for you when it felt like it. That was actually worse than becoming a shut-in or an agoraphobe. Just believing that no matter what, it might get you. So you might as well do whatever. He'd been hell on his parents during his teenage years.

And it had been hell on his soul.

Because it just... Everything felt tenuous. All the time.

But the stars were still there. He wasn't sure how many years it had been since he'd thought to look up at them before Shelby had just prompted him to.

It was a hell of a thing.

"I can see why they chose to get married up here. There's so little light pollution. I mean, I'm about to pollute it all with my flame in my grilling. But you know."

"The cost of progress," she said.

"True."

He put the steak on the hot grill, and watched as the flame rose up.

"Is there a salad or anything?"

"Of course. And baked potatoes. I did them before I came up. I'm not an animal."

"Well, that's kind of a revelation."

"There's one baked potato. We're going to have to split it."

"You brought up two steaks?"

"I don't take chances with steak," he said.

"Fair enough."

Silence lapsed between them. "This is very nice of you."

"Well," he said, shrugging as he looked down at the grill, "we are about to be family and all that."

"Not really. I mean *we're* not. It's not really like that."

"I guess not. But functionally it kinda feels that way."

She turned a small circle, then separated from him and went and sat down on the couch nearby. Her hands clasped in her lap.

"So," he said. "What is it you do exactly?"

She laughed. "What is it that I do?"

"Yeah. Your sister's an EMT, and you…"

"I make jewelry. I bead things. I sell a lot of it online. But… Yeah. You know. Things like that."

"Really?"

"Yeah. Do you not frequent the farmers markets around here?"

"No."

"Well. I'm very good. But mostly, I'm lucky to have family land, which I also work."

"Yeah. That is nice. I also benefit from that."

"And you're still riding…bulls?"

"I am indeed. Still riding bulls, and traveling around when I can."

"How long does a person do that? The bull riding thing."

He shrugged. "As long as your body can take it. Though, I admit it's not as easy as it used to be."

"What makes a person want to do that?" She was looking at him, something bright and mysterious burning in her eyes just then.

"Family business."

"And that's it? You do it because you saw the people before you do it?"

She looked a little bit disturbed by that fact. "Aren't we all doing that to some degree or another? I mean, it's easiest to take a path that you've seen forged, isn't it?"

"Maybe," she said.

"Why?"

"I don't know. I was feeling like maybe I'm not all that adventurous. But… You make bull riding sound the same as deciding to get married and have kids just because your parents did it."

"In a lot of ways, it's the same. You do this thing that seems like a legacy, I guess." But he felt a strange pang in his chest, and he didn't want to think too deeply about why.

"Except, you haven't done that part."

"No interest in it. So yeah, I guess it's not exactly the same. I knew how to get into the rodeo because it's the family business. But I don't have a whole lot of interest in the domesticity part. I have enough of it with the family I have."

"Makes sense."

"And you?"

"I think it's obvious what I wanted with my life, isn't it? I got married when I was eighteen. You don't do that if you don't want… That same thing. That thing your parents had. You don't do that if family isn't your dream. But I don't have it anymore. So… I guess maybe that's why I asked. How long you're going to do the bull riding. And when it ends, then what?"

"I don't know. And I'm not really sure I get how it connects."

"Because I'm living in this…*and then what* space. The first thing I wanted is gone. So what do I do now? And I don't know the answer."

He didn't know why she'd chosen to ask him that. Maybe because they were relative strangers. Maybe because he was something entirely different to her, and to her family. Maybe just because the steak was good, or because the stars were bright.

Maybe to scare him off, because she felt the same heat burning between them that he did.

Whatever the reason, he found himself wanting to give her an answer. And he didn't have one. He wasn't deep. Not by any metric. But he wished that he had something to offer her.

"Maybe that's the secret," he said. "Maybe nobody knows what to do with that second choice. Because the fact of the matter is, we all end up living with the less-ideal scenario at some point. Whether it's work or family or... We all have to face it at some point. And maybe you never quite know what to do with that part of your life as clearly as you knew what to do with the first part."

That cut close to his bone. But it had nothing to do with bull riding.

"Eventually everybody loses someone. And the older we get the more someones we lose. And you're always living in that and after. Always." He shrugged. "It takes away little pieces of the life that you knew. Of the things that you imagined. And the more of those pieces you lose, the more you have to rebuild. I'm not sure that the answers ever get clearer or easier to see."

"So what then?"

He looked at her then, and he noticed a necklace around her neck. Made with fine little beads. "Did you make that?"

"Yes."

He did something he knew he might regret, and took a step toward her, reaching out and touching the center of the necklace. "And how do you make something like this?"

"With a thread, a needle and these little seed beads and…"

"Right. But do you throw them all on all at once and see the big picture?"

"No. You go one bead at a time. But you have some idea about where you're headed."

"Right. But maybe in life sometimes we just have the one bead. We don't know how it fits into the bigger picture. So we just have to keep going. One bead at a time. One step at a time."

"I didn't realize that you were a philosopher," she said, her breath quickening as she looked up at him.

"Neither did I. But you suddenly made me want to try it out."

She cleared her throat and turned away. "Don't overcook the steak. I like it medium."

He cursed and went over to the grill, poking one of the steaks with a fork and slicing it so that he could get a look at the color inside.

"Not overdone."

He stuck the meat on plates, and they went back in the house, where he added the baked potato and salad. "Want to eat outside?"

She nodded.

They went back outside and sat opposite each other on the patio furniture, the plates in their laps.

"I guess my worry is that maybe it's not making a picture. I haven't done much of anything for the last few years. Maybe I haven't added a bead at all. You know. So to speak."

"Well, grief is like that. And that's different. You need to give yourself time."

"Right."

"You know about my sister."

"Yes. I do. I'm sorry about that. It's hard. I can't imagine what it must be like when it's a child."

"Loss is loss. You don't need to go ranking it. But yeah. I... She wasn't well for a long time. And I took care of her. We all did but... I just wanted to make her comfortable. And sometimes that was impossible. But it obsessed me. Distracting her, trying to do things to make her happy... And when I lost that, I didn't really know what to do. For me, that looked like a lot of years of bordering on juvenile delinquency. But eventually I figured that wasn't a very good tribute to Sophie. And that was when I got serious about the rodeo. And it just gave me something to do that was... That was something. I'm not going to say I made anything for the greater good, but it brought me closer to my family again. Because that's what we do. So it seemed like a worthy enough pursuit. I guess bull riding is my 'and then.' There will be another one too. Because I can't do it forever."

"How many new lives are we supposed to live?"

"As many as we need to, I guess."

"I guess."

They ate in relative silence after that. He couldn't remember the last time he had a conversation that was so… It brushed up against all the difficult things he preferred not to think about. And yet, he wanted to talk to her because she was asking him those questions. Because it didn't come from a place of gawking at pain, but of sharing it. Because she knew what loss was, and… And that was the thing. If he could make the loss of his sister mean something, he was always willing to take that opportunity.

If it could be used to help her, well, that seemed like a decent enough tribute. At least, the best he had.

When they finished up, they carried their plates inside and put them in the sink. It wasn't all that late, but Shelby picked up her bag and began to sidle out of the room. "So just… Any of the rooms upstairs that don't already have your stuff in them?"

"Yep. I took the first one, because I'm lazy. So any of the others…"

"Great." She walked slowly up the stairs. "Thank you. For giving me a place to stay."

"Thank you for… Eating dinner with me."

"Yeah. See you tomorrow."

"See you tomorrow."

And then she disappeared down the hall, and he couldn't help but feel that he had let an opportunity slip by. But he couldn't quite say exactly what it was.

Five

When she woke up the next morning, she was breathing hard. Because the lingering effects of the dream that she'd had last night were still making themselves known in her body. She was tingling. All over. Because there had been a moment downstairs right before she had gone up to her room when she had imagined what it would be like if she crossed the space and kissed Kit Carson. She didn't let herself have those thoughts. She'd had them, yes, but she considered them to be intrusive thoughts. In the minute she was aware of them, she shut them down. But he was under her defenses, and he had been nice to talk to, which was maybe the most surprising thing. And that had opened up this floodgate.

And her dream had been about a whole lot more than kissing. Her dream had been about scorching, hot, naked…

No. No. She wasn't doing that. She wasn't indulging it. Because she was going to have to go downstairs and head back over to the farmhouse, and she was probably going to see him. And she really didn't want to. She really did not want to have all this in her head when she did see him. That was going to make things impossible, and awful, and she really wanted to avoid impossible and awful.

So she got up, and got dressed, and shoved all of that out of her mind.

As she looked in the mirror, clipping a beaded barrette into her hair, she just stopped for a moment and stared at herself. Why had she shared all of those things with him?

It was being out of her house. Out of her empty house, and realizing that she hadn't done that in far too long. That her life was divided so firmly into this before and after that she had lost a lot of different pieces of herself. She didn't go out with her friends anymore. She'd done that when she was married. Had gone out sometimes with the girls, had dinner, had drinks. She had gone on weekends to vacation houses, and hung out and talked and laughed and ate food. She'd gone on dates with Chuck, and even though she wasn't… Even though she didn't have him, and even though she didn't really want to date, it just represented another thing that she had lost along with him. Because she had stripped herself down almost so she could focus on what she didn't have. Almost so she could hold the loss keenly against her chest and simply cling to it. Because who was she without it.

She hadn't known who she was without Chuck, and somehow that had morphed into her life being about the lack of him. And sitting in this completely different environment with Kit Carson, of all people, had spurred those questions. Maybe because she did know he knew about loss. And he'd been so surprisingly giving with what he'd said.

Well, don't go romanticizing it.

You think he's hot. You think he's hot, and that is a little bit dangerous.

She hoped that she would listen to her own scolding.

She shoved her pajamas into the duffel bag and went downstairs. And she didn't get a chance to breathe, didn't get a reprieve at all, because there was Kit, standing by the coffee maker, a mug in his hand.

"Good morning, sunshine."

"Good morning to you too."

"Busy day of wedding prep ahead," he said. "Though I figure we ought to check and see what's up with the power at your place."

"Yes. That would be good."

"Probably the fuse box."

"I wouldn't know where to find it or what to do."
She felt slightly embarrassed by that.

"I was married for a long time. My husband did
all of that. And now my dad does it because he feels
sorry for me and I lean into that."

He laughed. "I have to say, I kind of respect that."

"If you have to go through something terrible you
might as well take all the help that comes your way."

And she had shrunk her life so fiercely, down to
just her family, down to that house, that it seemed
fair enough to take all the sympathy that her parents
were willing to dole out.

The field was bright green in the daylight, the sun
illuminating each blade of grass, fiery-gold-tipped
green all around them. There were purple flowers
scattered throughout, and she wondered why it suddenly felt like she was waking up along with the
world.

Like she hadn't really breathed or seen these
things around her in the years since…

She looked over at Kit. And he was just as striking
as all the natural beauty around them. He was wearing a black cowboy hat, a black T-shirt. It outlined his
broad shoulders, his muscular chest and slim waist.
He was tall. She was tiny next to him. Chuck had
only been a couple of inches taller than her.

Kit Carson had always seemed like an entirely
different species to her. The kind of man who could
just as easily be on the silver screen, he was so much

larger than life. He was not the kind of guy you could say vows to, live a life with in a modest home. Dream of warmth and comfort and children with.

He was a mountain. And she was not a mountain climber by nature.

But then, that was the before Shelby, she supposed. She had never needed to climb a mountain.

Why are you thinking about mountain climbing? It sounds sexual.

Yeah. It did. But there was a part of her that was still humming with feelings that were decidedly sexual. So why not?

They didn't speak as they crossed the field. And the only sound when they approached the house was their shoes on the porch steps.

It was a stark contrast to the bachelor den the guys were staying in. It was white and delicate, with a wraparound porch and lace curtains.

The kitchen was all done up in a cheerful yellow, and it made Shelby imagine what it would be like if she lived in a different house. If her view changed. Or her life changed.

There was nothing holding her here. Not really. There was nothing holding her in place except herself. She could just start over. She could do whatever she wanted. She was still living like Chuck was in her life, but without any of the benefits. She had taken everything but grief from herself.

And it was just so… Starkly clear when she began

to imagine what life might look like. She tried to take a breath, but it was hard. Her lungs felt too small. Or maybe it was her that was too small.

Her life.

And Kit Carson was large in the feminine space, and he seemed to fill up everything. Everything around her. Everything she was.

"I'm going to check the mudroom for the fuse box." He slid past her in the kitchen, and her breath caught when his warmth and scent tangled around her.

She didn't take a full breath again until he was out of the room. And then suddenly, all the lights came on. "There," he said, coming in. "That was easy. Just had to find the one that was tripped."

"You probably could've done that last night," she said.

"Yeah. I could have. But then you wouldn't have been able to have steak with me."

She felt herself smiling, felt her cheeks getting warm. Was he flirting with her? She wouldn't even know what to do with that. She never flirted. Not in her life.

Guilt hooked around her insides.

Because he was a forbidden object. She had made him a forbidden object all those years.

It was why she was so antagonistic to him usually. Because what was wrong with her? She had the most wonderful man. He was everything. He gave her everything.

But Kit had always felt like sex and danger, and she hadn't trusted him.

Hadn't trusted him to care that she was married if they encountered each other in a bar.

And her deepest fear, her deepest unspoken fear, was that if he had ever drawn near to her... She would forget what mattered. She would forget that she had everything with the man at home. And throw it all out for this one burning, bright thing.

You wouldn't, though. Because you didn't. You never did. You never let him get close enough, it never happened. And it still hasn't. Not even after Chuck died.

So there. Her resistance of him, even now, was evidence of her purity. Of the fact that she wouldn't have done it. And it made her feel exponential relief. So there was that.

He might not be forbidden anymore, but her ability to resist him proved something. Something that mattered to her. Something valuable.

"I was going to go over to the barn today and start getting the favors in place and things like that." She looked down the hall toward where she had stashed all the baskets of things.

"I'm happy to help with that," he said.

"You don't have to."

"Yeah. I know. But you know what they say, many hands make light work and all of that."

And she really might as well say yes. Because truth be told, she enjoyed his company, and all of her issues that were swirling around inside her were her issues. So that was that. She didn't need to treat him like he was an enemy. Like she was afraid of him.

In fact... Why not be around him? Why not... Keep testing it?

"Great. I figured I would save some of the bachelorette party stuff, in part because I don't really want to live amongst the decorations."

"What?" he asked. "It's not your chosen decor motif?"

"I cannot say that it is. But, my house is more functional than decorative."

"I think I have the same straws at home."

"I don't think you do," she said.

He walked past her and into the hall, where some of the laundry baskets filled with favors were stacked. "Shall we carry these out to the truck?"

"I really should've left them. Instead of unloading them in the house."

"No big deal."

He grabbed them, in one stack, and stuck them in the bed of the pickup truck. Then they got inside the truck, and she felt a little bit less confident than she had before. In her decision-making.

Because suddenly being in such a tight space with

him made her feel… Warm. And made her feel very tingly between her legs.

This was dangerous. He was dangerous.

She swallowed hard.

"Let's go."

She was trying to untangle her own motivations. What if she wanted to test herself and see if she was pure? Or did she want to fail the test?

None of it sat comfortably with her.

She felt scratchy.

Very, very scratchy.

She wasn't used to having to figure out her motivations. She was just used to existing. Get up, help her parents with chores around the ranch, work on her beading for a few hours, watch TV. Eat sometimes in between those things. Visit with Juniper maybe. Her life was simple. This wasn't simple. And she didn't know what to do with this more complicated calculation of behavior.

It was a short drive to the barn, and when they got there, they pushed the doors open and found it set for the ceremony. There were chairs, and in the back part of the barn there were tables for dinner.

"Wow. I really didn't think Juniper would ever get married. She was more of a love-them-and-leave-them kind of girl."

"Chance wasn't any different."

"I guess it makes sense that they'd end up together, then. Similar mindsets. And neither of them prepared for it."

He chuckled. "I suppose so."

She and Kit were different. Shelby was a lifer. That was the problem. She had wanted to be committed to one person forever. It was her ideal. It was what sounded like life.

She didn't want to go to bars and hook up. Didn't want to get to know anyone. The idea of having to fall in love all over again was… It actually just sounded exhausting. She had married a man who had known her since she was a child. He understood her. Melding their lives together had been easy. And now she was firmly set in her ways, and… The very idea of trying to figure out how to shape her life around somebody new made her want to lie down.

So maybe she wasn't a lifer anymore. She didn't want to date particularly, for all the afore considered reasons, but… She didn't really want love again either. She couldn't even imagine it.

"I'm glad they found each other. Either way. Expected or not," she said. "It's a… It's a good thing for them."

"Yeah," Kit agreed.

She cleared her throat and started to get all the little tulle-wrapped bubble bottles out of the laundry baskets. With their glorious ribbon curls trailing from them.

"There's supposed to be one for each seat at the table," she said. "Because everybody is supposed to blow bubbles when they walk through to go cut the cake."

"That seems very fluffy for Juniper."

"Yes. But apparently the wedding has made her fluffy. At least, she's fluffy in regard to the decorations. I don't think she would appreciate being called fluffy in general."

"No, of course not."

They got them positioned on the table, and then she looked down the aisle. "There should be everything to put the canopy together in the back of the truck."

"A canopy?"

"Yes. She's going to walk under a canopy to go down the aisle. We made a frame for it and got some tulle to wrap around it. I know how it's supposed to go together. She didn't say that we needed to get it set up, but I think we could."

"Sounds like a lot of work."

"Well. My sister is being high-maintenance, and I guess she's entitled to it. She was the bridesmaid at my wedding, and it was pretty damned high-maintenance."

"So this is payback?"

"I believe it is payback in part, yes."

They went out to the truck, and she found the metal poles in the bed, and then she took the carefully wrapped tulle out as well, and with Kit's help they took it into the barn. She directed him, telling him where to lay the poles out in the aisle, because she had seen Juniper's sketches of it all.

She had done some beading on the tulle, just to add some sparkle. To add a little bit of them.

She had done the same for Juniper's veil.

"Is there something to anchor these?"

"Oh, right. I forgot. There's a couple of cement forms in the bed of the truck."

"I will get them."

He left, and returned a few moments later, with big cement bricks in his hands. The poles were meant to sit down inside them, and they held them in place. They were really heavy, and he made lifting them look like it was a breeze.

And she couldn't help but watch. The play of his muscles. His forearms, his biceps. She watched as he made every trip, and she just stood and kind of stared. Openly.

He was… He was glorious. Kit Carson was the most beautiful man she had ever seen, and she felt it was a traitorous thought, one that made her feel as much guilt as it did excitement. And it brought her back to her dream. Because in her dream, she had crossed the kitchen last night instead of retiring to her room. In her dream, she had put her hand on his face and kissed his mouth, and then he had put his hands all over her body. He had taken her against the wall, his arousal hard and thick and devastating, and she had screamed her pleasure in a way that she had always thought was fake, and found nowhere this side of ridiculously overblown in movies and porn.

And hey, it probably wasn't to be found anywhere outside of adult entertainment. Because she had dreamed it. It hadn't really happened.

She had certainly never experienced anything like that.

She shifted uncomfortably.

This was the problem. She didn't have experience in the sense that she had only been with one person. So her experience wasn't broad. But she'd had all kinds of sex. Years of it. Steady. Because she had been in a consistent relationship for so many years.

And when you were in a long-term relationship, you tried things. All the things.

It was such a scary line to walk. Because she had no idea what it would be like with someone else, but she also knew what was possible. And she really wanted to test the limits of what was possible with Kit. Or rather, her libido did. Or better, her more critically thinking self didn't want to do that. But sometimes when she looked at him, it felt like her critical self did not exist. It was just her replaced by a horny monster that she didn't recognize.

And again, she had to question what her motivation had been in doing this with him.

And why she was watching his muscles.

Did she want to resist? Or did she want to throw herself headfirst into something different?

Into something new.

"Can I help you with something?"

She blinked. And she realized she was standing there gaping.

"No. No. Sorry. I'm just… My sister is getting married. I'm just a little bit overcome. Emotions. I'm very sentimental."

She actually kind of was. She knew that most people wouldn't characterize her that way, but a woman who still had all of her late husband's belongings could hardly be considered anything but sentimental, she supposed. A woman who hand-beaded a bunch of details that no one would ever see, but she would know were there, could not be characterized as anything but sentimental.

"All right. Let's start getting this thing up." They started placing the poles, the supports and the different sections.

He found a ladder in the back of the barn, and they set it up, him working by stretching as tall as he could go and using the full length of his arms, and her needing the ladder every step of the way.

She showed him how the tulle was supposed to wrap around the frame, and she had to admit, he made a very skilled laborer.

"You would be handy to have around the house," she said, not thinking until the words escaped.

He looked at her, lifting a brow. "Would I?"

"To reach tall things. And open jars."

"I do know how to do both of those things."

"That's all I meant by it."

"I didn't think you meant anything else."

"Somehow I don't believe you."

"That is between you and your God. And not my concern."

"Everybody else is coming up today."

"Yep."

"I guess we better get that bachelor and bachelorette party thing ready."

"Definitely."

He took a step toward her, and she found herself scrambling back as if he had physically touched her.

He didn't react strongly, but it was the slight jolt in his frame that told her she had surprised him with her response.

"See you later, then. At the barbecue."

"Yeah. See you then."

And she had never needed to get away from another person so badly in her entire life. Especially not while feeling the intense desire to stay with him.

Six

Everybody gathered around the catered barbecue just outside the newly decorated barn. Family was here, and there were many friends thrown into the mix. The pre-wedding party was a big one, and he had a feeling tonight was going to be a pretty wild celebration.

But for now, the men and women were joined together having a potluck, and it was pretty damned good.

But he was still fixated on what had happened between him and Shelby earlier.

She had jumped away from him like his fingertips were on fire and he might burn her.

You know why.

Yeah. He could say that nothing had been happening. It hadn't been, strictly.

And yet, everything had been.

There was an undercurrent between the two of them that was difficult to ignore.

And need that was growing in his gut.

And it was complicated by the fact that their siblings were getting married, and she was vulnerable. He could see it. She was at a crossroads in her life, and she was looking for something, anything to hold on to.

And he was all right being a temporary mistake. Hell, maybe that was what she needed. But he couldn't be anything else for her.

So he needed to watch himself. And he wasn't all that good at watching himself. She was sitting with her sister, talking and laughing and eating, and he found himself a little bit overly fascinated by her.

"I can't believe how much you got done," Chance said. "You didn't have to do all the work. We were planning on getting some of it done tonight and tomorrow."

"Yeah. But I'm the best man. I wanted to do it for you."

"I have all these brothers. What good are they if they don't all help out?"

"Well, Shelby was in here doing it all, and I figured I shouldn't leave her to her own devices."

Chance looked at him, a little bit too sharp. "No. I suppose not. Awfully nice of you to assist."

He looked back over at his brother. "I think we both know that I'm not that nice."

"Yeah. So… Don't mess things up with my sister-in-law, please? She's been through enough."

Irritation stabbed at Kit. Primarily because his brother wasn't off base on things. But it was still offensive that he felt he had to tell him that.

"Yeah, I wasn't really planning on closing the loop in the family tree."

Chance chuckled. "Well. See that you don't. Honestly, the issue isn't… The issue is just that you and I both know that you don't want anything permanent. And she's been through a lot."

"Who hasn't?"

"Good point. Look, man, if the opportunity comes up for a little bit of fun, and that's what she wants, that's different."

"Are you warning me away from your sister-in-law, or are you giving me permission to have a one-night stand with her?"

"I'm actually not doing either one. You're both grown people. She gets a say in things. I am expressing my preference for you not making my life difficult."

"Got it. You don't want your wife to get mad at you."

"Correct. Or, my wife's grandfather, who scares the ever-loving shit out of me."

"Fair. Look, it's nothing I didn't think of already."

"How long have you two…?"

"Nothing's going on between us."

"No, I get that, but you're into her."

He shrugged. "I just think she's hot."

"Right. Well. Hey, whatever. Things are set up for camping tonight?"

"Hell yeah. Epic camping. It's going to be great."

"Good. After we play pool."

"Of course. We gotta make use of the house too. I just figured a little bit of sleeping in the woods was also in order."

"You thought of everything."

"I try to."

And he realized how true that was. He did try to think of everything. To the best of his ability. He tried to take care of everyone. Protect them.

He just knew how desperately short a person could fall with those things. And it haunted him. He had a feeling it always would.

But tonight was about celebrating his brother. Sending him off into a new life.

Kit might never be able to see having a new life of his own, but he could definitely be happy that Chance would have one.

Definitely.

The party in the farmhouse was raucous. Luckily, their mother hadn't planned on staying in the farmhouse for this part, which was good, because if she had, they all would've died of embarrassment.

The alcohol was flowing freely, and Juniper, their friends from school and a couple of the EMTs whom Juniper worked with were all giddy and lessening their inhibitions. Shelby had opted for sobriety since she was running the whole show, and felt like she wouldn't be a great host if she let herself get too loose.

Are you just afraid of imbibing too much with Kit in the vicinity?

Well. It didn't matter if Kit was in the vicinity or not. He was out with his brothers, so it didn't matter. She was safe. They now had a buffer of all these people.

Still. Keeping her wits about her was probably the better part of valor.

But Juniper was living it up. She had her phallic crown placed on her head, and had a bright pink drink with a straw of the same color.

"This is immature," she said, lifting her glass to Shelby.

"I know," Shelby said. "That was the idea."

"Well, excellently done," Lydia, one of Juniper's friends, said, reclining back on the couch and laughing.

They had all put on club dresses, as if they were going out for a night on the town, and not just sitting in a farmhouse playing games with a group of women. But it was fun. Shelby hadn't done anything like this for a long time. It was fun to dress up just for herself. Just for a group of women. She had gone a little bit overboard. She was wearing a short emerald green minidress that had lived in the back of her closet for at least ten years. It did not fit the way that it once had, and her more generous curves made the hemline ride up higher, and it clung to her breasts and her stomach in a way that made her self-conscious now. Except... She looked at herself in the reflection of the window just quickly. If she saw it on another woman, she would think the woman looked great. So why she was being hard on herself she didn't know. Maybe it was just that harsh reminder of the passage of time. That she wasn't an effortlessly willowy teenager anymore, and that she didn't have a husband who just loved her through all the changes.

Love yourself, then.

That was the point of tonight. All the women were dressed up, just dressed up to please themselves in this group.

And yet, Kit was on her mind.

She really needed to get a grip.

This night reminded her a lot of her own bachelorette party, and she felt guilt at the way she seemed unable to separate Juniper's happiness from her own all those years ago. Maybe it was normal. Maybe it would've been like this no matter what. It was just that it should've felt happy, and not ominous.

Not strange and sad. This heavy reminder of the ways in which life can take unexpected turns.

She suddenly felt outside of the festivities. Being the sober one probably didn't help.

"Next game," she said.

She moved quickly into explaining the rules of the card game that had them matching up certain phrases with other phrases, creating the most outrageous combination that they could.

It quickly had everyone dissolving into fits of laughter, and she had beauty queen sashes with dubious honors printed on them to pass around to the women she deemed winners.

It was going on one in the morning, and they had music pumping, and everyone started dancing.

And Shelby couldn't escape that feeling that she was just… Standing outside, looking in. Participating, yes, but not really there also.

She could remember so keenly the night before her wedding.

Young and so filled with hope for the future.

And then… And then they'd been married. And it had been good. But there had been hardship. Figuring out how to pay bills in this small town, how to get enough work to cover it all, while knowing that they were lucky they had the house on her parents' property to fall back on.

The fact they hadn't been able to get pregnant, and didn't have health insurance so they hadn't had the luxury of going to a doctor and finding out why. They just kept hoping it would work.

It was supposed to. They were young, and they were healthy. And hell, they'd spent their teenage years trying desperately not to get pregnant, doubling up on all manner of contraception to make sure that it didn't happen before they were ready, and dammit, why couldn't it happen when they were?

They'd been happy still. It was just… She was ready. For that next part of her life.

They'd been saving. Saving enough money to go and get answers. To figure out what they needed to do. And then the accident had happened and…

She blinked, suddenly coming back to the moment.

It was like she had been watching a movie of her own life. From the night of that party to tonight. And it was… Jarring. To come back to this. Her sister was just starting down that road now. And Shelby had already walked on it.

She hoped it was better for Juniper in ten years. She really did.

But she suddenly just felt old, and like she really wasn't part of this for a reason.

There were no more structured games happening, people were just dancing, and she had a feeling they were all going to get sleepy soon.

She melted into the background of the room, and then slipped quietly out the back door. It was warm outside, not as hot and sticky as it had been inside, but pleasant, with a cool breeze blowing over the field.

She closed her eyes and let it wash over her as she walked off the porch down into the grass.

She felt tears slip down her face, and she didn't bother to wipe them away.

It was just a moment by herself. Just a moment to let all of this wash over her. Wash through her.

Just a moment.

And when she opened her eyes, she saw a figure, dark on the velvet blue horizon. And she knew immediately who it was, standing one hundred paces from her, with the bachelor pad to his back.

She didn't say anything. She just stood there, regarding him. He knew it was her. She didn't need to ask.

They had both left their respective parties.

She wondered why he had. Wondered why tonight was too much for him.

She took a step toward him, at the same time he took one toward her.

Until they had closed almost all the distance between them.

And she didn't know what she should do. If she should speak, or if they were past words.

They had talked last night when talking wasn't what either of them had wanted, and she'd known it. They had talked today, when all she had wanted to do was look at his fine form.

Sure, there was a lot of talking that could be done. A lot of concern about consequences and fallout.

Disclaimers and things like that. But she had a feeling they both knew them. That they both lived in the pocket of the same sorts of concerns and there was no reason to put voice to them. No reason to break the spell of the moment with language that could never capture what was happening inside her anyway.

The truth of the matter was she wanted Kit Carson.

She had wanted him when she was a middle school girl and he was in high school, standing across the field from her looking like everything she had never thought she'd ever see in real life. She had wanted him as a grown woman, her heart firmly engaged in her marriage, her vows happily and meaningfully spoken. She had looked at him and seen the promise of desire fulfilled in a way she had never imagined. And she had turned away from it, because she had promised she would. Because love outweighed desire.

She had wanted him amid all the dark lonely days since, and hadn't even let herself fantasize about him because she was still testing herself. And why?

Suddenly, it was like she had let go of a burden that she'd been carrying all this time.

Why. Why was she still carrying it? What was she trying to prove? Why was she still trying to be... Strong? To be better? Why? What did it matter? What did it matter what she did? What did it matter whom she was with now? Her house was empty, her bed was empty. He was dead. Death had done them part. That was it, it was the end. And she wanted so badly in some ways for it to not be the end that she just couldn't…

But Kit was here. And she was so tired of being better than this fire that had ignited itself in her veins all those years ago.

She wasn't better than it. She was it. Entirely. Utterly. And tonight she wanted to burn.

She was the one who made the move. She knew that she would have to be. It was a fraction. A breath. But he saw it for what it was. And suddenly, she was in his arms. Strong and certain and hot. His chest was a wall of muscle, and she pressed her palms flat to it, felt his heartbeat raging there. He was tall, so tall, and she was disoriented by the height difference, but in the best way. She felt small and fragile, but it didn't undermine her. She was so used to being strong because she had to be. And right this moment, it didn't feel like she had to be. It didn't feel like it at all.

It felt like he was holding her up, it felt like he was holding her in place. It felt like he might be holding all the world on those broad shoulders, just for a moment, just for her.

She smoothed her palms up and down, feeling the hard delineation of his pectoral muscles and reveling in the answering kick of need between her legs.

Yes. She was a grown woman. And she knew what the hell she wanted.

She wanted Kit Carson.

No explanation. No apologies.

No disclaimers.

And he seemed to be of the same mind.

And just when she thought she might die of the frenzy that was whipping up inside her, he lowered his head. And finally, finally that hard, uncompromising mouth was softening over hers.

It was demanding, and he parted her lips roughly, sliding his tongue against hers as if he was voracious, hungry. Starving.

She whimpered, wrapping her arms around his neck and pressing her breasts flush against his chest.

And then she felt herself being lifted off the ground, like she weighed nothing, and she supposed to him maybe she did. And all of her insecurities from earlier tonight just melted away. Because her body fit against his. Because the years had changed her into the sort of woman who could withstand this. Because the years had brought her to this moment. Stripped away everything that had ever prevented it whether she wanted it to or not.

She was here. And she was the woman whom she was. The woman who could have it.

So she had to honor it. The changes. The aging. The weight. The loss. She had to honor it, because it was why she was here. And she couldn't hate herself, or second-guess, or warn herself off about consequences.

Because it was like this moment had been destined to unfold from the beginning.

And she refused to feel guilt over that thought either.

If the moment felt like fate, she was going to take that too. Because no one had asked her if this was what she wanted. If this was where she wanted to stand. If she had been able to pick her own life she would be back at home with her husband and the children they'd had years before, but she had been denied all of that, so she would have this. Unreservedly.

She would have it.

For the Shelby who stood here now. The Shelby with the thicker ass and thighs and rounded stomach. That Shelby. The Shelby who had loved and lost and felt so broken she didn't think she could ever stand again.

The Shelby who had always done the right thing in the face of temptation because doing right and being right and loving right had mattered.

But now only this mattered. Not tomorrow, and not yesterday. Only this.

And he was everything. Everything she had never allowed herself to fantasize about and more.

His lips were hot and all-consuming, and she felt his kiss burn through her like a wildfire. Burn through her without compromise.

She throbbed between her legs, excitement blooming in her midsection, her breasts growing heavy. Her nipples demanding his touch.

She had never kissed another man. And yet, it felt like because it was Kit it just fit.

And it was a good moment for it. For him. Because she knew what she wanted. She knew what to demand of him. She knew where she wanted to be touched and how.

And suddenly, he moved his big hands down her back, down to cup her ass, and he squeezed her hard, commanding and possessive in a way she never experienced, and she realized that even if she might know what to demand, there were other things that he knew.

And suddenly, that feeling of inexperience, the lack of understanding of how he might touch her. Taste her. Of what he might choose, made her feel giddy with excitement and nervous like she was a virgin.

Because she knew where this was going. Wherever they had to go. Wherever they had to go to make it happen, she knew that this wasn't ending in the field. That it wasn't ending at a kiss.

With her legs wrapped firmly around his waist, he held her and began to walk back toward the bachelor house.

"You should put me down," she whispered, breaking the silence for the first time, and she regretted it. Because she had broken it with her uncertainty, and she didn't want to bring uncertainty into this.

But he did nothing but chuckle against her mouth, the way his breath filled her causing her to shiver.

"I'm good."

She realized that they were going into the house. "Everyone's camping," he said as he walked them up the porch, and she disentangled her legs from around his waist, feeling a little bit silly that he was carrying her like she was a koala bear.

But all he did was lift her up fully into his arms, opening the door and closing it behind them, before kissing her hard right there in the entry, deep and unending.

"This is what you wanted, right? You didn't want steak. You didn't want to banter with me about ribbon curls, or just stand there watching me drink a beer. Or even have me open yours. This is what you wanted."

She nodded slowly. "And it's what you wanted too."

"Back before we even had a situation," he said, the words rough and ground out.

And the explosion of desire that ignited in her was too all-consuming to deny. "Thank God," she said, and she grabbed his face and kissed him. With everything she had. With everything pent up and brilliant in her.

She kissed him. She kissed him because she didn't

have another choice. She kissed him because he was everything. She kissed him because if she didn't she might die.

And then she realized they were moving again, that he was carrying her up the stairs.

"Good thing you chose the closest bedroom," she said.

He laughed, but it sounded strange. He pushed the door open, and then slammed it shut behind them, pushing the lock. "Just in case. You never know who's going to wimp out and try to use the indoor plumbing."

"Or notice that you're gone," she said softly.

"They are pretty wasted," he said. "And there are a lot of us."

"Yeah. My sister and her friends were pretty wasted too." She blinked. "You're not wasted." She just needed to check. Because if Kit Carson needed to be drawn to have sex with her, that was a little bit embarrassing.

"Haven't had a drop."

"Me neither."

And right then, as they stared at each other in the dimly lit room, she wondered if that was why neither of them had had any booze. Because if they were drunk, it would've dulled their senses for this. Would've created a gray area where one of them might have wanted to refuse because the other one was compromised. Or, they both could've been sloppy drunk, but then they wouldn't have remembered it. And there was one thing she knew for certain. This was her only shot. Because it was complicated, and neither of them wanted that.

This was just the fulfillment of a fantasy. And it was one she really needed. Because she was trying to find a way to move on. Trying to find a way to make a change, and this was it. It was what she needed. But it wasn't going to be a regular thing.

It was a singular gift that she was giving herself before she decided… If she was going to move. To change her scenery forever. To get herself out of the echoes of the life that she had before.

So yeah, she wanted to be present for it. And like he was reading her mind, he reached out and flicked the lights on. It was bright. Bracingly so, but she understood. He wanted to do this with everything lit up. With no mystery, with no fuzzy edges. And she found it was what she wanted too.

"Take your clothes off, Kit Carson," she said. "Because I have been wondering what was under them for far too long."

His mouth quirked up into a grin, and he set her down slowly on the edge of the bed. Her heart hammered at the base of her throat, throbbing insistently.

She shivered as he reached up and began to undo the buttons on his shirt. His chest was well muscled, covered with dark hair, and she squirmed in her seat, as her center throbbed, moisture flooding her, because she was just so damned hot for him.

Women weren't visual her ass. She could get off just looking at Kit Carson.

He shrugged the shirt off his broad shoulders, and her mouth went dry.

He was masculine perfection. His abs would have been highly regarded back when her family had first settled the area. They could've cleaned their clothes on them.

And he had those lines, narrowing down beneath his jeans, pointing down to that part of him that had hardened into an insistent bulge pushing at the front of his denim.

She moaned. She couldn't help it. And he laughed. But not her. He slowly undid the buckle on his belt, undid his jeans and kicked his shoes off as he shrugged his pants and underwear down. As he revealed the whole rest of his body to her, and damn. Just damn.

She had really never. Not even in her wildest fantasies. He was beautiful. Thick and long and just gorgeous. She had a healthy appreciation for the male form in general. She liked the look of a naked man.

But she liked the look of this naked man better than she had ever liked anything in all her life.

And then he did something wholly unexpected. He knelt down slowly on the floor in front of the bed, and looked up at her. The expression in his eyes was wicked, the curve of his lips a sin.

He smoothed his hands up along her thighs, beneath the hem of her dress. And he found her panties, grabbing them and dragging them slowly down, removing them, but leaving her shoes still. Then he moved his hands to the insides of her knees, parted her legs, and she felt her face ignite as he examined her, his expression one of filthy awe.

"Do you have any idea," he said, "how long I've wanted to taste you? You make me so hard. Do you know that? Do you know that I fantasized about you? I have a policy. I don't do the married-woman thing. Sorry. But it's been that long. And you tested me."

"Well, I didn't do the infidelity thing. So it's a good thing you didn't try."

"But now it's all good. And I have wanted you… I have wanted you."

He pushed her dress up, exposing her completely, and his gaze only seemed to get hungrier. Then he kissed the inner part of her thigh, and she started to shake.

She couldn't believe it was him. Kit Carson. Right there. Looking at her like that. Like he wanted to devour her.

And she knew he was going to. All of her nerve endings were at attention. Her whole body on high alert.

His mouth moved higher, pressing soft kisses on

her thighs, and then, then, he put his mouth right over her, her center, and she let out a short, shocked sound, because even though she had known it was coming, the reality of it was just so much more. His mouth was hot and confident, and his tongue went deep inside her before he slid it over the most sensitive part of her, then sucked her deep into his mouth. He shoved his hands beneath her ass, and brought her hard against him, as uncompromising here as he was everywhere else.

And she lost herself. In the way his shoulders held her legs wide, and the rough feel of his fingers, digging into her flesh. And the white-hot pleasure that his mouth gave her. She lost herself utterly. Completely. She clung to him, and she felt her climax, quick and impossibly intense, building inside her, and she wanted to resist it. Wanted to stop it. Because once she had one, she wasn't going to have another, and she had really wanted it when he was in her.

But there was no fighting it. It was too good. Too enticing and tempting, so she let go. And she couldn't help it. She screamed. She rolled her hips in rhythm with the waves of pleasure that were moving through her. He rose up on his feet, growled and grabbed hold of her hips, lifting her back farther onto the bed as he covered her. He ripped her dress down, and then off completely, throwing it onto the floor. She was still wearing her shoes.

He kissed her. And she returned the kiss, wrapping her arms around his neck and giving him everything she had. He covered her, his chest hair rough against her breasts. And she moved her hands all over his body. His chest, his back, feeling all the muscles there, down to his ass. She parted her legs, encouraging him between them. And she could feel the hard press of his arousal against the entrance to her body. She moaned, rubbing against him, slippery with need, but he didn't give her what she wanted. Not quite yet. He lowered his head, and took her nipple into his mouth, sucking hard.

And she ignited.

He sucked her hard, and she wrapped her legs around his, arching against him, trying to assuage the ache between her legs. She was so close. Again. Already.

"Please," she whispered.

And then he thrust home.

She gasped. He was so big. And she hadn't been with anyone in a while. Years. So it was a little bit of a shock.

Sex toys were not Kit Carson. He was bigger and more. Hot and insistent. And he was in control.

He grabbed her hands and held them up over her head as he began to establish a steady, hard rhythm that rocked her. Utterly. Mercilessly.

She looked up into his eyes, looked right at his face. The lights were on. And she wouldn't let herself forget. As if she could have.

She was with Kit. Kit.

And then, it was like everything around her was fire, and so was she.

Her climax ripped through her. Her need overcoming her as she cried out his name. As she felt wave after wave of desire pulsing through her.

And then he growled her name on his lips as he shuddered and shook. And if there was one thing that was better than finding her own release in Kit's arms, it was watching him find it in hers.

This man, the object of her darkest and most shameful fantasies, was surrendering to her.

To them. To this.

It was everything. He was everything.

And they were something else entirely.

And when it was over, she lay there, sweat-slicked, her heart pounding so hard she thought it was going to escape her chest.

"Oh, well," she said.

Because it was all she could say. They weren't wrong. They weren't exaggerating, those movies. You could lose yourself, lose your head. End up screaming and not care who heard you.

It was a revelation.

One she had always been a little bit afraid she could only ever have with him.

And there it was.

"Good for you?"

"Extremely," she said.

They lay there, and she looked at him, at his body.

And she was sad. Because she could've… Well, she could want this for a long time. She could want this forever.

That made something like an alarm bell go off inside her. She wasn't supposed to be thinking things like that. Wasn't supposed to be thinking in those terms. Because there was no point to it. None at all. They both knew what it was. "Thank you," she said. "But I really should get back. Because…"

"I know. Same reason I should."

"You know that this can't…"

"I think we both know exactly what this was. That's why we didn't talk about it beforehand, right?"

She nodded. "Yeah. So… I'll see you at the wedding tomorrow."

He nodded slowly. "Yeah. See you at the wedding."

Seven

It was tempting to be smug when he was the only one who woke up the next morning without a hangover. Except... He couldn't say with confidence that he didn't have a hangover of some variety. Of the Shelby Sohappy variety, in point of fact. Because that woman had turned him inside out. Had left him completely wrecked.

He had had a whole lot of sex in his life, but he never had anything quite like that.

He couldn't explain it. It was just her. The look of her, the feel of her, the taste of her.

"Hey, assholes," he shouted, experiencing a great amount of satisfaction when all of his brothers groaned.

"Chance is getting married today, so you all better deal with the hangover situation."

"Do you think yelling at us is going to help?" Boone asked.

"I'm not trying to help."

"Why are you not hungover?" Chance asked.

"Superior genetics?"

"We have the same genetics."

It was his brother's day. He should be thinking of best-man things and being responsible, maybe even being happy perchance, but instead his mind was firmly fixed on the events of the night before. Of Shelby, and what it had felt like to finally touch her. To finally kiss her. To finally be with her. She had been everything, and they had been incendiary. It had been more than he had ever imagined being with her could be, and he had imagined quite a bit. She had been a revelation. There had been a connection between them for years. An ember that had burned bright, and last night it had exploded into a flame that had threatened to consume them both.

He knew that he was the first man she'd been with since her husband's death. He felt that. Like it was a weight to carry, a burden, and yet, he couldn't say he minded. Not really. If someone was going to be that man, it was better that it was him. Because he had wanted her for a hell of a long time, and there had been nothing he could do about it.

Well. Not again. And today they needed to focus

on his brother and her sister. That's what it was all about.

So he rousted those idiots he called brothers, and got them fed, got everybody's suits ready to go.

Boone looked at him as he finished tying his tie. "Where were you last night?"

"What do you mean? I was with you."

"You see, I wasn't all that drunk. I noticed you leaving. And I noticed that you didn't come back for a couple of hours. So, where were you?"

"Maybe I was working on a surprise for Chance."

"Yeah. Maybe you were. Maybe you were working on a surprise for Chance, and that's all legit. But… I have my suspicions."

He narrowed his eyes. "Do you, now?"

"I do. I think that you found the maid of honor."

"And why do you think that?" he asked, his voice flat. Dangerous.

"Because you want her. Because you have wanted her for a record number of years. I think we all know that."

"That's interesting that *you* know that, Boone. Because *I* don't know that."

"Liar. Fucking liar. You want her. You know it. And I think something finally happened between the two of you."

"I think that I didn't ask for your opinion, Boone. That's what I think. So maybe you should take a little bow tie and get ready to go stand at the front of the church. Otherwise, we might recast you. You would make a charming flower girl."

"I would," Boone said. "I'm happy to tiptoe through the tulips anytime. But none of that deflects from the fact that I think you're a liar."

"Well. That is brotherly love, isn't it? You think that I'm a liar. What an asshole."

"Yeah. I'm an asshole. But hey, don't worry about it. I'm sure that Chance would be thrilled to know that you hooked up with his sister-in-law."

"Chance doesn't need to know. Does he?"

"Is that a confession?"

"You think what you think. What does it matter what I say or not?"

"Nothing. Just…"

"Yeah. I know. Be careful. Be careful with her because… All those reasons."

"Yes. All those reasons. Unless you're about to make like Chance and get everything together and make forever…"

"I get that you think she might want forever, but she doesn't. Not with me." He wasn't anything like her husband, and he didn't want to be. He wasn't ever going to be a forever guy, and if her past actions indicated anything… She was a forever type of woman. "That was just old business. Needed to be taken care of. It had been deferred way too long. Believe me. She doesn't want forever. She's had that.

You know how it is. You lose someone… Nothing is ever the same again."

Boone got a faraway look in his eye. "Yeah. I know that." He cleared his throat. "I also know sometimes you…miss your chance with someone and regret it."

He didn't know what his brother was referencing, but it was clear something else was going on with Boone. And also that Boone didn't want to go into detail about it, or he would have.

"It wasn't about having a chance for me. It was just attraction."

"Whatever. I hope you had a good night."

"I fucking did."

"Good, then. As long as all involved were satisfied, I assume the day will go off without a hitch."

"It's not my day. It's Chance's."

"True. True."

And he kept that in mind as they assembled for the wedding. Kept it firmly in mind when the bridesmaids showed up. Kept it firmly in mind when Shelby, wearing a red dress that scooped low and showed off her stunning breasts, came to stand near him, because they would be walking down the aisle together.

"Hope you slept well," he said.

"Just fine."

"Did they notice you were gone?"

"When was I gone?" She looked at him with unfathomable dark eyes.

"Guess you weren't."

That was how they were going to play it. Like it hadn't happened. Even though they both knew it had. Even though he had a feeling they were both replaying scenes of the night before as they stood there regarding each other.

"Yeah. I know."

They linked arms, and walked down the aisle, taking their place where the bride and groom would stand.

The wedding was beautiful. Went off without a hitch. And he was glad. He was glad for Chance. Because the man deserved some happiness.

And Boone was right. Unless Kit was willing to make changes—big changes—unless he was willing to abandon his entire life, he had to leave Shelby alone. He just did.

But it looked like Shelby was more than willing to leave him alone. At the reception she danced with just about everyone but him. A knot of jealousy formed in his stomach, but it should be gratitude. Gratitude for the fact that she knew what had happened between them was temporary.

He just wished it was more than once.

Maybe. But it wasn't.

And when they saw Chance and Juniper off, away from the barn, away on their honeymoon, he should have felt glad. Grateful.

Because their little dance together was done. Because the families could go back to being about as distant as they'd ever been. They would see each other occasionally. But not all that often.

Yeah. This was over. He had scratched the itch that was Shelby Sohappy.

And he should be glad that it had gone off without a hitch.

Shelby couldn't believe it. She really could not believe it. In a deep, profound way that had her ignoring the problem for four whole weeks. Until it happened again. She hadn't seen Kit Carson since the wedding. She had been telling herself that she was fine with that. But all the while, there was a growing unease, a growing sense of disbelief that had taken root inside her. She had a feeling it wasn't the only thing that had taken root. But it didn't seem possible. She had tried to get pregnant for years. Granted, she didn't really know what the source of her inability to conceive with Chuck had been. She had known that it could have been him, but she had just felt like the odds were with her. Women's bodies were tricky things. And it had seemed reasonable that the issue was her.

Yeah. It seemed completely reasonable, completely standard, really, that the issue would be her. They hadn't gotten to find out yet, though. And then in the end they hadn't. But this was two missed periods. Two. And that was two more than she had ever missed in her entire life.

She'd never been pregnant. Not once. She was as regular as cows that needed feeding, and there was no doubt in her mind that this missed period was not a coincidence. How could it be? How the hell could it be? And she knew that what she needed to do was talk to her sister. Confess everything. Figure out what the hell she was supposed to do. She wanted a baby. She had wanted a fresh start.

Those two things hadn't really gone together in her mind. Because, of course, she had wanted to be a mother in context with the marriage she had with Chuck. She hadn't really considered being a single mother. But here she was…

You don't know if you'll even be able to keep it. Eight weeks. It's not secure yet. You could just leave it. You could just keep ignoring it. You could not talk to anyone about it.

Except, she was already dialing her sister. Already time to find out where she was. As an EMT, Juniper was often on call, or in the far reaches of Lone Rock and the surrounding areas.

"Are you around?" she asked without introduction.

"Yeah. Pretty around. Are you at home?"

"Yes. I need to talk to you. I mean I really need to talk to you, and I need you to not tell Chance."

"Well, this is a little bit disconcerting. And I'm not sure what to do with it."

"Come over. Don't make any promises yet... Just come over."

Shelby started pacing. Pacing the halls of this house that still had her husband's clothes in it. It had been a whole thing coming back home after the wedding. Sleeping in the bed that she had shared with her husband, having gone to bed with some — one else. And not just anyone else, Kit Carson, who had been a source of guilt and shame for her for all these years.

She had known that she needed to make a change, and she still hadn't done it. She had just sat in whatever all this was. Had just sat in her... Her funda— mental misery, and she still hadn't made a move. Maybe this was her move. Maybe it was an answer to prayers that she hadn't had a voice for, hadn't had concrete words for.

"I'm here," she heard her sister call through the front door.

She scrambled back to the front of the house. "Thank God."

"What the hell is going on, Shelby?"

"I think I'm pregnant."

"Holy shit," Juniper said, staring at her.

"Yeah." She chewed the edge of her thumbnail. "I know."

"*How* pregnant?" Juniper asked, her eyes narrowed.

FREE BOOKS GIVEAWAY

GET UP TO FOUR FREE BOOKS & TWO FREE GIFTS WORTH OVER $20!

We pay for everything!

See Details Inside

it today to receive up to 4 FREE BOOKS
and FREE GIFTS guaranteed!

She felt heat creeping up the back of her neck. "Why is that the question?"

Juniper's expression went granite. "I think you know why."

Shelby coughed. "Well, that would be two months," she said.

"Coincides with my wedding date, doesn't it?"

"You can't tell Chance yet."

Juniper looked too all knowing, and it hurt. "Kit's the father?"

"You know he is," Shelby said, feeling defeated and seen and helpless. She knew that Juniper knew. That was the thing. Maybe that was why she wanted to talk to her sister more than anybody. Because she just already knew. And no matter how much Shelby had ever tried to deny it, Juniper had known that Shelby was attracted to Kit.

"You're pregnant though," Juniper said. "Really."

"I haven't taken a test. I've never missed a period. In all the time that I was married, and we tried. We were trying to have a baby, but I never got pregnant. Not one time. I was never late… Nothing."

"You didn't think about protection with Kit?"

"I didn't think about *anything*," she said, throwing her hands out wide. "If I had stopped to think about anything, I probably wouldn't have done it."

That was a lie. But it made her sound a little bit more thoughtful. A little bit more balanced and sane. So she was going to go ahead and go with that.

"Right. Well. You have to tell him."

"Why? He doesn't want… He doesn't want to have kids. He doesn't want to settle down."

"Neither did Chance."

"I don't think that I'm going to be able to contrive to give Kit amnesia so that he can forget all of his trauma and fall in love with me." Just saying that made her cringe.

"Anyway. I'm not in love with him. He's… He was this vaguely bad object that I had in my life and I… I don't know that I want to get married again. I don't know. I don't think that I love anyone else. I loved Chuck for all of my life. And it was special. I had this… This weird thing with Kit. And I hated it. I've never really known him, I've never especially liked him, and I just wanted to tear his clothes off. From the minute I first saw him. It's never been okay with me to feel that way. It's never been what I wanted. This thing with Kit has never been what I wanted. I do want a baby. I was even moving away, Juniper."

"You can't do that," Juniper said. "You can't give me a little niece or nephew and then move away."

She realized when she said that the moving thing wasn't feasible. Or fair. Moving away when she was having a baby. What would her parents think? Her grandparents? Well. What the hell were they going to think when they found out she was pregnant without a husband? That was the whole thing. It was a whole damn thing that she hadn't thought she would be dealing with when she was twenty-eight years old.

"Kit needs to know," Juniper said. "You need to give him a chance to do something."

"He's a Carson. He's an alpha male. What do you think he's going to do? He's going to storm in here and try to take over my life."

"So, tell him no. You're an alpha female, Shelby. And you know that. Why are you acting like he's going to run you over? He's not. You've got to handle this with honesty. You have to."

"Why?" Shelby said, knowing that she sounded petulant. "Why do we have to be grown-up about this?"

"Because you're going to have a baby. Maybe. The first thing you need to do is take a pregnancy test."

"Do you know if they expire?"

"I… I don't."

"Well, I have a few. In the bathroom. I was just avoiding them. I've been avoiding everything. I've been trying to pretend that it didn't happen. That all of it… Just didn't happen."

"Very healthy. But, it might be time to take a different approach. But I'm here. If you want someone here. I can also go if you don't want me here."

"I'm afraid to know," Shelby said.

"What exactly are you afraid of?"

"That it will be positive. That it will be negative."

The idea made her want to burst into tears. Both of them. Seeing the results at all.

"Well, it's going to be one of those things. I'm sorry. That's just… A fact. But you want to know, right? So that you can start figuring out what you're going to do."

"I don't want to." She was about to say something along the lines of she had been working way too hard to figure out what she was going to do for too long, since she had been thrust into a change she hadn't asked for. But she hadn't been. She had just been sitting. She hadn't chosen to lose Chuck. It wasn't the consequence of anything. It was an accident. A car accident that had changed her entire life in the blink of an eye.

But this… This was her fault.

This was the direct result of her actions. It was… She'd slept with Kit without a condom. And she had put herself in the situation, and just suddenly that felt a little bit powerful. She wasn't sure she would ever be able to explain that to her sister. Because it sounded a little bit unhinged. But… This was her life. It was a choice she made. To be with him, to not take precautions. So… Here she was. At least she was doing something. Even if it was just a reaction to something else she'd done. She had earned this.

This moment, positive or negative. It was something new. It was, in a very messed-up way, that step forward that she had been avoiding taking. And now here she was taking it.

"Okay. I guess I'll try one of the tests that I have."

"Okay. I'll wait for you."

With shaking hands, she went into the bathroom, and got one of the tests. She had taken so many pregnancy tests. In spite of the fact that she never had a late period. She had done it just because she had hoped. She had kept them on hand just in case. But they were good for three days before a missed period, and she had kept them and taken them three days before more than once. And now they had just been sitting there for a couple of years. No reason to be taken.

It was such a strange, familiar routine. But in the past, she hadn't had a missed period. In the past, even though she had hoped, she had been certain of the outcome. She was not that certain here.

And when two pink lines came into view for the first time in her damned life, she could not believe it. She swallowed hard and exited the bathroom.

"It was positive," she said, standing there looking at Juniper, trying to gauge her expression.

"Oh, Shelby. You want this, though. I know you do. You want a baby."

Suddenly the intense misery that overwhelmed her was almost too much.

"I wanted my husband's baby," she said, her eyes filling with tears. "Why didn't we get to have that? All those years, and we didn't get pregnant. I didn't get to give this to him. He died and he never got to have it. And I'm… I'm going to do it without him. Because I had sex with someone else. Because I…"

"You're still alive, Shelby," Juniper said, crossing the space and taking her face in her hands. "You're alive. You're going to move on, you're going to do things that Chuck couldn't do. And I know it's not fair. I know. I loved him too. He was like a brother to me. Shelby, when I came upon the scene of his accident, when I had to tell you… It was the worst day of my life. It is still the worst day of my life. There is nothing that will ever match that. It was hell. We both went through hell. But you're alive. And he isn't. So yes. You're going to have sex with other people. You're going to smile again. You're going to be happy. You're going to feel good things and bad things. And if you want to, you get to be a mother."

"I could still lose this pregnancy."

"You could. But you could still be a mother if you choose to be. You could still adopt, you could get fertility treatments until it happens. It's your life, Shelby. And nobody gets to tell you how to live it. And it doesn't have to stop. It doesn't have to stop just because you lost somebody. You don't owe him a half life."

"But it feels like I do."

"I know."

"And that it's Kit's makes it even worse."

"Why does it make it worse?"

She wanted to hide from that question. But she

knew hiding was over. "Well, first of all, I can't keep it from him. And second of all… I feel guilty." She looked away, her throat aching. "Because it is wrong to be attracted to another person when you're married."

"No, Shelby. It's wrong to act on it. And you didn't. You never did. You can't help that you and Kit have physical chemistry. You could help what you did in response to it, and you did the right thing. You always did the right thing. You were good to Chuck. You were appropriate in your response to Kit. And you don't have anything to feel guilty for. You can't help your feelings. It's what you do with them."

"The sex was so good," Shelby said, breathing out hard. "I knew it would be. I knew it. I can't… I can't love him. I don't want…"

"Then don't. Don't. Like I said. It's your life. But if I'm going to strongly push you in any direction, it's to be honest with him. He is my brother-in-law. I cannot lie to Chance about this. I know who the father of the baby is, and I can't pretend that I don't. So… That just has to happen."

"I'll tell him," Shelby said. "It's another thing I don't really want to do. Or deal with. And that makes me a little bit tired."

"That's understandable. But you know, I did a pretty messed-up thing with Chance, and you called me out. I didn't let you in on my plans before I did it. If I had, I probably would've made a different decision because I would've seen the look on your face, and know that I couldn't lie to him like that. So let me be your conscience now. You've got to tell him as soon as possible."

"I need… I need a favor first."

"What is that?"

"Will you help me pack everything up here? I need to change the house. I need… I need new stuff. I need to get rid of the old stuff. Because it's been way too long, and it's starting to feel wrong. Really wrong. It's starting to feel creepy. I can't tell Kit that I'm pregnant with his baby with Chuck's clothes in my closet, okay?"

"Yeah. I can help you with that. I'll let Chance know I won't be home for a couple of hours."

"Don't tell him yet."

"I won't. I'll let you talk to Kit first. Just because I think that's the way it needs to go."

"Thank you," she said. "I really appreciate it."

And then, she and Juniper set about to make the clean slate that Shelby should've made for herself a long time ago. And it felt like more, like better than she could've imagined. Even though the sense of dread looming before her seemed nearly unmanageable. But all she could do was put one foot in front of the other, just slowly. One thing at a time. One piece of clothing at a time. One wedding photo at a time.

And she left one. Hanging on the wall, right in the center. Because there were fresh starts, and then there was ignoring the past in a way she simply couldn't. She would always be shaped by her marriage. By loving Chuck. She wasn't going to pretend otherwise. No matter what. And even though she felt steadfastly cowardly at the moment, that felt just a little bit brave. So she would take that. Cling to it. She didn't really have another choice.

Eight

It had been a fairly normal day. He had only thought about Shelby and what she looked like naked five times. Before coffee. So it was going well. He had thought about her maybe ten times more in the hours since. She had wrecked him. He hadn't been able to get excited about another woman since then. Hadn't even really bothered. He'd considered it one night at the Thirsty Mule when he had gone down to have a drink with Jace, but had abandoned it pretty quickly.

But hell, there was no reason to obsess about her.

What he needed to do was get back on the road. He had been flirting with the idea of retirement from the rodeo, and had been picking up more responsibility on the family ranch. He liked it. Liked the idea of being here with his brothers more. He had decided to take this season off. And yeah, he figured that was probably one foot in retirement. But he was in his thirties. He might be avoiding that "and then" stage of things, but he was definitely there.

He looked across the landscape from his vantage point on the back of his horse, flat and rocky, scrub brush as far as the eye could see. This place was home. And he tried to imagine it being home in a more permanent sense. He hadn't been settled ever. Even when he'd been a kid, they'd gone around the circuit along with their dad, staying in an RV when they could. They'd only ever had stability when Sophie had been ill. And even then, it hadn't been a real stable sort of stability. Having a sister in and out of the hospital wasn't stable. Having a sister die wasn't stable.

His phone buzzed in his pocket, and he reached into it. He had a text from Jace.

Shelby is here to see you.

And suddenly, his blood went molten. Maybe she had been thinking about him too. Maybe she was here to... Maybe it was just as bad for her. Maybe one time wasn't going to be enough. *What the hell is wrong with you?*

He didn't know. And he wasn't going to allow that

question to land all that deep. Because he wanted what he wanted. He wanted her. And he was clear on that.

So he urged his horse into a flat-out run, the dust coming up high, rocks and clumps of mud all stirred up in his wake. And when he came up to the front of the barn, Jace was standing there, alongside Shelby, who did not look like she had come for afternoon delight. Or indeed, delight of any kind. Her expression was flat, something steely reflecting in her eyes. Her lips were turned down. It didn't make her any less sexy, not to him. She was still a pocket-size package of absolutely everything he wanted in a woman. But she didn't look like she was here for what he wanted.

"I need to talk to you," she said.

"Yeah. Sure."

Jace looked at him with cool speculation, and Kit curled his lip and lifted his hands, giving his brother an expression straight out of their childhood.

He could tell that Jace wasn't going to let him off all that easy. But for now, he was going to have a talk with Shelby.

"The barn?" she asked.

"Sure. If you want."

"We need to talk alone."

"It may have escaped your notice, but a lot of people live here. Alone is kind of a tall order."

"Then let's… Go for a drive."

"Okay."

He walked over to where his truck was parked, just in front of the barn. "Care to get in?"

"Sure."

His brother was handling his horse, and Kit started the engine of the truck, heading out toward the remote part of the ranch where he had just been. He drove over to the edge of a ravine, the view down below of mountains that looked like they might as well be made of moondust, red and yellow and black paintbrush strokes. It was beautiful. Still not as pretty as her. Even when she was... Well, she wasn't glaring. She was just not looking at him.

"What's going on? I've had a lot of strange interactions with you, but none of them have been silent."

"I have something I have to tell you. And I don't really know how to do that."

And just like that, the view in front of him seemed to go sideways. Suddenly the mountains were to his right and the sky was to his left, and he didn't even know where his stomach was. Somewhere. Because there was only one reason for a woman you'd slept with to say words like that to you.

"Fuck."

"Oh, you guessed," she said.

"I need to hear you say it."

"I'm pregnant."

"Yeah. Well." There were spots in front of his eyes. A baby. A damned baby. And suddenly, all he could see was Sophie. Small and vulnerable and sick. Dying. And there was nothing he could do. The crushing weight that he felt every night when he went to bed. The need for her to be better. The knowledge that she wouldn't be.

And he just never... He never wanted to feel those things again. He never wanted to feel responsible for that sort of thing again.

He turned and looked at her. Hell. She was pregnant. Pregnancy was not an altogether safe condition. And so many things could go wrong. For her. For the baby.

"Have you been to the doctor?"

"No. I just took a test. I suspected... I suspected about a month ago. But I didn't want to jump to any conclusions. I've never been pregnant before. And I've tried. So... I didn't actually think that I could."

"Shit. I didn't even think about protection. I didn't even..."

"I didn't either," she said.

"It's not your fault. I mean, it's not your fault entirely. It's mine too," he said.

"Well, how generous of you to acknowledge your part in a process that I would be physically incapable of completing on my own."

"I'm not suggesting that I'm being heroic in taking responsibility. But you can't deny that some men don't or won't. And I'm not that guy. I'm not going to blame you or say that you should've said something or done something different."

But there was panic rolling through him. A sense of horror that he couldn't seem to shake, a sense of urgency. He needed to do something. He needed to take control of this somehow.

"I had to tell you, because I told my sister, and she can't not tell Chance. She told me there was a very tight clock ticking on that."

"Would you not have told me otherwise?"

She was silent for a long moment. That silence told him a hell of a lot.

"I don't know. Because I was thinking about moving away. And I feel like that offer still needs to be on the table. You don't have to be involved in this. I've wanted a baby for a long time. This isn't how I saw it happening. I told you. I didn't see it happening this way at all. I didn't think that I could. But I wanted a baby. I wanted to be a mother. You don't have to be involved. You can consider yourself an anonymous sperm donor."

"Like hell I will. Like hell I will. I'm not a sperm donor."

"What are you, then? We had a one-night stand, Kit. A one-night stand that might've been a long time coming, but you don't owe me anything. You and I do not owe each other anything. It was sex. Nothing more."

"I'm the father of the baby." And as soon as he said it he realized it was true. "The father, do you understand? Not a sperm donor."

"Do you want a child?"

"It's immaterial. I'm having one. That's how it is for me. I can't have a child walking around on this earth and know about it and not claim him. Bottom line. That's just how it is. For me, that's how it is."

He hadn't wanted this. Hadn't wanted this worry, this burden or this responsibility. But it was here, it was happening, and he couldn't contort it into something else. There was no way. Absolutely no way at all. For him, it wasn't a matter of whether or not he decided to step up. He would.

"I could still lose it."

"But it's here now."

And suddenly, the silence seemed to swell between them. The enormity of that. The reality of it.

Even though it was barely the promise of a heartbeat right now, they had... Made something together. It couldn't be nothing. Not to him. It could not be nothing. "We should get married."

"No," she said, the denial abrupt and sharp.

"Why not?"

"Because it's not 1950, you dope. We don't need to get married. This is not a reason to get married."

"It's about the only reason I can think that I would ask a woman to marry me."

"Well, I'm flattered. How many women have you had to propose to?"

"None. You've never been pregnant before. I've never gotten anyone pregnant before. I don't generally…or ever, have sex without condoms. It was very important to me to avoid this. I didn't. In this case. So… I think marriage makes the most sense."

"I've been married, Kit," she said, her voice suddenly soft. "We didn't have a baby. And we were married. Husband and wife. Childless the whole time. Kids are not what marriage is. Marriage is about loving somebody. Being in a partnership. Marriage is about choosing *them*. Not… Some version of a family."

"I think marriage can be either thing. Sometimes people get married for that reason. Sometimes people get married for convenience. Sometimes people get married for kids."

"Not me. Not me. I will never get married for less than what I had before."

And he didn't know why, but that stuck in his chest. More than a little bit. But he couldn't argue with her. Not really.

"I'm moving in with you, then."

"No," she said. "There's no reason to do that. I could have a miscarriage. Something could go wrong. I don't even have the baby."

"So we can move in together after you have the baby."

"Or we share custody. Like grown-ups. Or we decide what it looks like then."

All these things were foreign to him. And none of it was making sense. None of it was clicking. He wanted her with him. All the time. He wanted to protect her. He wanted to keep an eye out for her. He wanted to keep surveillance on the baby in utero and out constantly. To make sure that everything was fine. To make sure they were safe. How could he keep her safe if he didn't have her with him?

"No. This is not going to work for me. You need to move in with me, or I need to move in with you. This has to... This has to be my choice."

"No," she said.

"I can't guarantee that I'm not going to fight you for full custody if you don't do this."

"Well, I will sic your brother on you. And I'm pretty sure I'll win that fight. Because Juniper and Chance are going to side with me."

And there was the entanglement working against him in a way he hadn't quite envisioned. His brother was accountable to her sister. And he had a whole bunch of threats inside him all bottled up. A desperate bid to control the situation, and he couldn't do it. He couldn't do it, because she wasn't wrong. His brother would tear him a new one. Or just remove the part of his anatomy that had accomplished making the baby in the first place.

"Well, I'm going to be at your house. Every morning. On your damned doorstep. Making sure you're okay."

"Why are you being a nightmare? Why don't we get to know each other?"

"Because I don't want to get to know you. You're the mother of my child."

"It is a zygote, Kit. Calm down."

"No. I will not calm down. Because you can twist and spin situations in life all you want. And you can try to avoid thinking about the logical, reasonable outcomes of things, and you can try to live in denial, but it does not change anything. Believe me. I've done that. I tried it. I tried just…being positive and happy for my sister when she was dying and… trying to be optimistic. It doesn't change a damn thing. When shit comes for you, you have to deal with it. You have to be realistic."

"I'm realistic. Don't talk to me now like I've never lost anything. Don't talk to me like I don't understand that life is difficult. I do. I do. I know how hard things can be. You know I know it. You know I do."

"Shelby," he said, suddenly feeling like there was a boulder in his chest. "I don't see it working where the two of us are trading a kid back and forth on the weekend."

"It has to. Because that's the only thing that I can deal with. Kit, it's all there can ever be."

They sat in silence for a long time. "We'll see."

"This isn't a negotiation."

"And that's where you're wrong. Because it isn't just your life anymore. And it isn't just mine. We are going to have to figure out what's best for this kid. And I'm going to argue my position on that."

And he could see that he had stumped her there.

"So what now?" she asked.

"Let's schedule a doctor appointment."

"Okay."

"I'd like to be there."

"I can't argue with that."

"I think you could. I think for some reason, on this, you don't want to fight me."

He looked at her profile, and he saw tears welling up in her dark eyes. "Well, maybe I don't want to be alone."

"Good. I don't want to leave you alone. That's not how this should be. It's not what I want."

"I'll let you know when I schedule one."

"You going to talk to the rest of your family?"

"Yeah. I guess I have to."

"Would you like me to go with you?"

"Would you like to be a Kit-skin rug on my grandfather's floor?"

"Hey," he said. "I offered to marry you. You turned me down."

"Yes, but you did have sex with me outside the bonds of holy matrimony."

"And you had sex with me right back," he said.

"Point is, I think you should maybe not be there."

He did not like this. This woman's insistence on independence. And it wasn't because he didn't respect an independent woman. It was because it all felt… He wanted to pick her up and wrap her in a blanket and carry her around. He wanted to make sure that she was safe, that the baby was safe. It all suddenly felt so fraught and fragile he didn't know what to do.

And yeah, part of him thought… It would be easier if this wasn't happening. It would be easiest if something went wrong now.

But there was another part of him, a large part, the biggest part, in fact, that couldn't cope with the idea of something going wrong. It would be one loss too many. It would be unfair. Unendurable. He didn't want her to go through that pain. He didn't want to go through it again.

So you're gonna be a dad.

If he hadn't been sitting down, the idea would've brought him down to his knees. It was unfathomable. He had never thought about being a dad. He had shoved that thought way to the side if anything even remotely resembling it had come up. Yeah. It was not his ideal.

He didn't know what to make of it now.

"I actually need some time by myself," she said.

"Are you brushing me off?"

"Yes. I am. Because today has been a lot."

"I don't deny that. But don't you think that you and I should… Talk about this more?"

"I already told you, I don't feel secure enough in this even being a thing to worry about that just now. We don't need to be picking out preschools, or whatever you're thinking."

"I was not thinking that. But thanks."

"I assume you're going to tell your family?"

"I have to tell my family. Because of Chance."

"Fair point. I understand that."

"Right. Well. Since we're not doing it together, I expect I better drive you back to your car and let you get on with things, and then I'll get on with things." He didn't like it. He didn't like any of it. But he didn't really have a choice either.

He put the truck in Reverse, turned around and started to head back toward the barn. Started to head back toward where Shelby had left her car.

He wanted to do something. Wanted to kiss her. But they didn't do that. *You weren't going to be doing things like that. Yeah. And since when do you just take things lying down?*

He didn't. And he wouldn't. As she got into her car to drive away, he began to put a few very concrete directives in place. He was going to prove to her that it was better if they were together. That it was better if they made a family. He was never going to be her late husband. He was never going to mean that much to her. But they could have another version of a family. And he was going to prove that to her. Even if he had to seduce her around the idea.

Nine

"Well. He asked me to marry him."

"Good," Juniper said. "If he had done anything else I would've hung him out to dry and..."

"I said no."

"What?" Her sister's voice was a shriek in her ear.

"I said no, Juniper. I'm not going to marry him just because I'm pregnant."

"Okay. Forgive me. But I don't understand why not. Because you want a family, Shelby..."

"No. I wanted a family with the man I was married to. We were a family. I am not in love with Kit." The words stuck something tender and hollow at the center of her chest.

She wanted to cry all of a sudden. She had made

it through that whole thing with him mostly without crying. Mostly. And she just couldn't…

She couldn't. This was too hard. It was scraping against things she didn't want to examine. It was making her… Feel things.

She hadn't even been tempted to say yes to him for a second, though. Because the idea of Kit and marriage just didn't go together. The idea of taking the thing that they were, this wild, untamed thing, the sharp edges that made her feel exhilaration and shame all at once, and pushing them into the life that she'd had before… She just couldn't imagine that. Of course, she couldn't quite imagine him being a father.

The father of her child. She had spent a lot of time imagining herself being a mother, and in that picture, she was soft. Sitting in a rocking chair, holding a baby. She was a different sort of woman.

Definitely not the woman who had climbed all over Kit Carson and encouraged him to do dirty, incendiary things to her in that bedroom.

That was not the woman bursting with maternal instinct who wanted more than anything to nurture a child.

That woman had been a moment out of time. A moment of insanity. A moment to inhabit a different reality.

That woman could not be the one who took control now.

She looked around her house. Small and humble. She tried to imagine Kit filling the space.

She couldn't. But then, she had no idea what her life was now. She had no idea what she was doing.

And she had a feeling that she wasn't going to find answers anytime soon.

But the sad thing was, there was a timer ticking on her getting things sorted out now. A timer growing in her womb.

So sort things out she was going to have to do. Starting with her family. Kit Carson was a problem for another day.

All his brothers were assembled at the Thirsty Mule. Well. All except for Buck. But that was normal. Another shitty normal in the Carson family.

This was all of them now.

It had just so happened that they were all available. He hadn't actually purposefully put the whole squad together for this announcement. And really, he probably should've first told his mother, who was going to be so thrilled about having a grandchild she wasn't going to be able to deal, but that was part of the problem. She was going to want to see Shelby. She was going to want assurances that the kid was going to be around all the time. And frankly, he had no such assurances. So, his brothers were going first.

"Surprised the old ball and chain let you out of the house," Jace said, slapping Chance on the back.

"The old ball and chain is on call, and was also exhausted after a day working the ranch. She's got too much pride to let me pay for everything, so she's just still working her ass off. But you know, I like that about her."

"That she's stubborn?"

"Yeah. Believe me. It's one of her better attributes."

And unfortunately, Kit knew exactly what his brother was getting at, since he had tasted the steely determination that family had. And found that it was very good indeed. Though, it was also a source of irritation for him right now.

"It's good," Kit said, "that all of us are together. Because I have something that I need to tell you all. So it's probably best that I only have to do it once."

And it was probably good that Chance's wife had been working, or the whole story would've been blown already.

Jace looked at him with no small amount of suspicion on his face. But then, Jace had been there when Shelby had shown up today.

"Yeah. So. There's no easy way to say it. But… I'm…" He didn't really know how you were supposed to announce this. He was having a baby? He was going to be a dad? And so probably the worst iteration of that came out of his mouth. "Shelby is pregnant."

"Dammit, Kit," Chance shouted, practically crossing three bar stools to get near him. "You knocked up my sister-in-law?"

"Yeah. I did. So… There's that."

"Juniper is going to kill you. Hell. Does she know?"

"She does know. She just wasn't allowed to tell you until I knew, and it turns out she's been working since then, obviously, or you would know."

"When did you find out?" Chance asked.

"I know when he found out," Jace said. "That'd be about three hours ago."

"Yes it would. So it's not like it's a secret that's been being sat on for a hell of a long time. Except Shelby has known for about a month. But she didn't tell anybody. But she confirmed it today."

"Right," Chance bit out. "Because of course you fucked her at my wedding."

"She fucked me back. So, maybe dial your umbrage down a little bit."

"Are you going to marry her?"

"Well, Chance, I offered. I offered like the salt-of-the-earth, code-of-the-West motherfucker that I am. And she said no."

"Of course she did," Chance said, snorting.

And he was a little bit surprised to hear his brother ruefully accept that. Except… His brother got it. That was the thing.

"You know you can't tell them anything," Kit said, meaning the Sohappy sisters in general.

"Yeah. I do."

"And because of you, I can't go hard-line on it."

Chance nodded. "I can see that."

"So unless your wife can talk some sense into her…"

"My wife is better at inciting violence than talking sense, and again, I like that about her, but I just don't know that she's going to be the one for this."

"Damn," Jace said.

Boone shook his head.

"So what are you going to do?" asked Flint.

"Well, I'm going to go on the offensive. I'm going to prove to her that she can't do this without me."

"That's what you want," Jace said.

"I'm having a kid. I wasn't going to do this. It wasn't going to be my life. It wasn't going to be what I chose to do. But it's where I'm at. You know as well as I do that sometimes shit just happens."

"Though in this case," Flint said, "shit happened because you didn't wear a condom."

"Yeah. I am aware that I have responsibility in this."

"You know we are here for you," Chance said. "No matter what."

"Thanks. Now if you'll be there to be a buffer when we tell Mom…"

"She's going to be thrilled," Flint said.

"Yep," Jace agreed.

"The real buffer you're going to need," said

Chance, "is when we tell Callie. Because she's going to read you the riot act."

"I can take it."

From his perspective, right now, he could take just about anything. Except having the situation left unresolved with Shelby. That he couldn't take.

But he was going to take charge of that. Immediately.

Ten

Shelby woke up, but she didn't get out of bed. She just lay there, the reality of her new life rolling over her.

She was pregnant. She was pregnant with Kit Carson's baby. There was no denying it.

And the sharp knock on her door seemed to underscore that.

Maybe it was her mom, coming to yell more.

There had been a lot of yelling last night.

It had all ended in tears. And everybody was fine now. She wasn't really surprised at the way that it had gone. They didn't want her to be a single mother. But they were reacting to stigma from a different time. And they were also acting like she was sixteen

and not twenty-eight. She had the means to manage
herself. She didn't care if anybody judged her. And
anyway, they weren't going to. It just wasn't like that
anymore. But they could not quite understand that.
She understood. They were reacting not just because
of the way the world was with women, but specifically because of the way the world was to Brown
women. She got it. She had lived her whole life in
her skin. But she was deciding to do this. And she
was assured in that. She wasn't a kid. She wasn't
doing this naively.

And she knew that her family would support her
no matter what. They would rally around. It was just
they had to air their opinions and grievances first.

And so sitting through the grievances had been
a thing.

But she had endured it. And now… Someone was
here for round two.

She was not quite ready for round two. Even if it
involved smothering and apologies.

She rolled out of bed, and padded to the door. She
pushed her hair out of her face and jerked the door
open, and froze. Because there was Kit Carson. On
her doorstep. Holding bags of groceries.

"What are you doing here?"

"I came to make you breakfast."

"I don't recall…" But he was sweeping past her,
into the house, and she felt as if he had broken an in-

visible tape that had been stretched across the door. Like he had breached something. Changed it.

Because here was this man in her house. This man whom she had slept with. Who was not her husband.

And he was getting food out and setting it on the counter. And rummaging around for pots and pans.

"Coffee?"

"I'm not sure on the coffee rules with pregnancy. I think I can have one. But I might just do tea."

"Works for me. But I need some coffee. Will the smell bother you?"

"No," she said, watching, feeling dazed as he opened up a package of bacon and put a skillet on the stovetop. Her stomach growled.

He turned with his broad back to her, and she couldn't help but admire his form. His muscular shoulders, his narrow waist.

She really needed to get a grip.

But there was bacon. And Kit, and things felt very confused.

"I don't know if you like bacon. Or if you prefer sweet breakfast. But I figured I'd do up some pancakes also."

"I… I like food," she said.

And she felt grateful then that she didn't feel any sort of nausea. Because that, she was given to believe, was a hallmark of the early stages of pregnancy. And she really had felt… Mostly fine.

She had felt a grim sense of foreboding, but she hadn't been sick. Or even really fatigued.

Suddenly, she wondered if that was something she should be worried about.

Well, this was going to be a joy. Worrying about not feeling bad was certainly something she hadn't anticipated.

"What exactly are you doing, Kit?"

"I told you. I told you that I was going to try to bring you around to my way of thinking. I wasn't kidding. I also told you I was going to be involved."

"Well, I don't really think that I'm open to your way of thinking."

"I don't care. And I said this isn't going to be a one-way street. Sorry."

"I don't actually think you're sorry."

"Look," he said. "There's no point in us fighting." The bacon began to sizzle in the pan, and her stomach growled.

"I don't know about that. Maybe there is a point to us fighting. We don't agree. So… It seems to me like there might be a reason for us to fight."

"There's not. We've got some time to sort this out. But I could be here. In the morning. I could take care of things. I can take care of you."

She looked at him, and there were sharp edges to the feeling that swelled within her. How was she supposed to agree to that? To the level of domesticity that he was proposing. How was she supposed to just… Believe that it would work?

It was like agreeing to let a tiger live in your house. Reasonable. Or indeed possible. That was the thing. She looked at Kit and she just didn't see how any of this was possible. Or how it could ever be.

"I've been taking care of myself for a long time."

"I get that," he said, taking a mixing bowl out of her cupboard—how was he finding things so unerringly? She could swear that he was better at maneuvering around her kitchen than she was. "But there's more to it now. There's a baby on the way. And you don't have to do this by yourself. You don't have to do this alone. So why should you?"

"Because, Kit. Because things change. And people die. And I don't even know how all this is going to work out. And jumping into it like this… I'm sorry. But it terrifies me." Admitting that made her feel small. Weak and pale, and she didn't want to feel like any of those things. She wanted to be a brave warrior woman. Somebody who had stared one of the worst things ever in the face and come out stronger.

Right now, she just didn't know how she was going to cope with all of this. "We just… We just don't even know how all of this is going to pan out, and it scares me, frankly. It scares me. Okay? I just can't…"

"Yeah. It scares me too," he said, stopping and turning to face her. "I get it. I know how fragile things can feel."

Except she wanted to tell him it was different. It was all fine when they were talking about grief in vague terms together. He had lost his sister. She had lost her partner. The person whom she was building her whole life off of. It wasn't fair. But that was the thing about grief. It wasn't especially fair all the time. And sometimes she wanted to lash out at people when they told her they had also lost somebody. She wanted to say it wasn't the same. That they hadn't grown up with their husband. That they hadn't loved the way that she did.

Yeah. It wasn't fair. It wasn't fair at all. But sometimes she just… She just didn't want to be fair.

"Well. You're not carrying a baby. So I don't really know that you do know how fragile things can feel. Right now… It all feels precarious. It could go away. It could go away, it could just not actually be happening. And that… I can't make plans with you right now."

He turned away from her, and went back to the business of making pancakes. The bacon was still sizzling. The domesticity of it made her head hurt. Made her chest hurt.

Because this wasn't real. This was him trying to get his way. And it wasn't… It wasn't right either way.

"You're right. I'm not carrying the baby. I'm trying to help you carry a couple of things. I get it. I'm not even your plan B. I get that. But you know, I'm also not a total deadbeat. And I'm trying to prove that to you."

"I didn't say you were a deadbeat."

"I know you didn't. But I'm also not the person that you figured on doing this with. And I get the feeling that you're more comfortable with the idea of doing it by yourself because it affords you a certain level of denial."

"I did not ask for you to psychoanalyze me."

"No. It's freely offered. Lucky you."

"And what about you? Because I don't for one second think that you're doing anything in a way that isn't also just about protecting yourself. Because that's what we do. All of us people. All the time. We want to protect ourselves."

He paused again. And this time, when he turned to face her, his expression was improbably grim. "Yeah. You're not wrong about that. Here's the thing. I want to keep you safe. I want to keep the baby safe."

"You can't just do that."

"This makes me feel like I'm close to it. And I need that. Okay?"

"Do you actually…? Would it be easier for you if it all went away?"

"Maybe. Maybe, actually. But I don't want that either."

And neither did she. Because yeah. It would be easier if this particular baby went away, and if she wanted to have a baby she could just go do it with a turkey baster, and actually commit to the single-motherhood thing. But she didn't want that. Because in so many ways Kit Carson felt like her destiny, and while she couldn't explain it, standing there resisting it as hard as she was, this felt a little bit like destiny too. Or maybe she was just trying to find more excuses for the fact that he made her behave like a wanton. Either way, this was complex in a way she really didn't want. And yet, it was the reality.

"I don't either."

He nodded, his expression hard, and then he turned back to the pancakes. She was silent while he finished cooking breakfast. And she didn't have it in her to be stubborn enough to turn down the glory that was this home-cooked meal. Because it really did look good.

"So… Do I want to know why you know how to cook breakfast? Is it that guy thing? Where you have to know how to do it, because you have a lot of one-night stands?"

"No," he said, snorting. "My one-night stands never stay for breakfast, Shelby."

She scoffed. "But you do have them."

"I have, yes. And you haven't."

"Just you." Heat sizzled between them and she did her best to ignore it. "Here you are. At breakfast."

"Here you are. Having my baby."

"Here I thought I was having my baby," she said. But the way that he looked at her, and the way that he'd said it, sent a shiver through her that had nothing to do with maternal instinct. It was that biological insanity that had brought them here in the first place.

"Mine too," he said.

"Right. Well. I guess so."

"If you enjoy the breakfast… There's plenty more where that came from."

She swallowed hard. "I think there needs to be some ground rules."

"Well. Let's go over the rules while we eat."

He dished up the breakfast for both of them, and she let him. Because it had been a long time since someone other than her mother had done anything like caring for her.

And she had to admit that she did enjoy it. A man moving around her kitchen. In her house. In her life. But the more she was trying to turn her thoughts right side up, the more she had to really think about the implications of this. He needed to be in her child's life. In their child's life. It was what he wanted. It was important to him. And that meant that they were going to have to be civil. More than civil, they were going to have to deal with each other. The passage of time. The way their lives might change. Proposing that they stay separate was safe in a lot of ways. Things would never be worse between them than they were now. They wouldn't allow for it to get sticky and toxic.

Sure, there was the unknown. Whether or not he would marry someone else.

She didn't think that she would.

But...

She ignored the cramping in her stomach that came as a direct result of that thought.

He wasn't really the marrying type. And anyway, if he ever became the marrying type, that was his business. She just felt possessive about it right now because... Well, she was pregnant with his child. That gave her the right to be possessive, didn't it?

It was just a temporary state of being. While she housed part of his genetic material. So there. That seemed like a logical place to put it.

He set the plates on the table, her mug of tea. And she sat in front of the plate, across from him, her heart thundering harder than she would like.

"We have to keep this like this," she said emphatically.

"Excuse me?"

"We're almost friends. And I think that's probably the best place for our relationship."

"We're almost friends?"

"Yes," she said. "We had that really good conversation the night before the bachelorette party..."

"And then we had sex the night after. So why is one of those things a bigger deal than the other? Because it seems to me, the sex is actually why we're here."

"It seems to me that that is an instructive lesson in the nature of sex, and what it can do to a relationship. So I'm thinking that we don't do that again.

That's what I'm thinking. I'm thinking, no sex. Because sex caused a whole lot of problems." She felt herself getting warmer and warmer each time she said the word *sex*, and she would really like to be done with that. But she had to act like it didn't matter, because she had to act like maybe they could be friends, because she needed that to be true and real and what was going to happen, because she had to get some control in the situation. She didn't have any, that was for sure.

And she needed it. That was one thing about grief. It had kept her isolated. But it was her grief to deal with and nobody else's, so while people were occasionally on hand to try and be there for her, it was essentially an all-by-yourself sort of thing.

And… She preferred that. This was joint. A partnership. With a man whom she didn't actually have a relationship with. Yes, she had long-standing avoidance of him because of her desire to see him naked, and then they'd talked, and she found that she quite liked him. And then they'd had sex, and she had found out she quite liked his body. But this was different. They had to be different. She clung to that image in her mind. The soft, sweet maternal life. Where she sat in a rocking chair and held the baby, and felt complete. Yeah. She tried to sit with that. For as long as possible.

"We're going to share custody of the child. And have to see each other. And right now, this feels good. It feels companionable."

"Companionable?" The way he asked that, low and flat and gravelly so that it echoed between her thighs, made a liar out of her, but she couldn't afford to let him know that.

"Yes," she said. "Pleasant, even. Why shouldn't we be able to share breakfast with each other? We should, right? This would be ideal. You could come over, we can have a meal. We get a family dinner sometimes. We could share custody, but also share a life."

"There's a thing for that. It's called marriage."

"No. That's disastrous. If we get married we're going to need very specific things from each other. It's going to be about us. This needs to be about our child. And so... No arguing. No sex. None of that."

"No sex."

"No."

"You're cool if I go have sex with other people?"

She ground her back molars together. "Totally fine. I have no claim on you. We are going to be a *Modern Family.*"

"What if I told you that I'm not predisposed to very modern ways of thinking?"

"Then I will tell you to go find some enlightenment. Climb to the top of the mountain or something. Commune with nature. Eat a Twinkie. Do something to reach an elevated state of being."

"What if I told you this doesn't work for me?"

"I don't want to fight with you," she said, feeling

like she was tearing strips off herself even while she talked, showing the ugly wounds she carried, showing her deepest self. She hated it. "I desperately don't want to fight with you. Because my life has been a series of fights with everything that has happened to me, with everything that is going on in the world, with… My whole soul for two years now, and I am tired. I am just tired of the relentlessness of it. And I need this to not be hard."

"I hate to break it to you, sweetheart, but I think having a kid is hard. I think change on this level is hard."

"I don't want it to be," she said, the words coming out choked. She just wanted something nice. Something good. She just really wanted to be happy. "I don't want it to be. I think you're a good guy. I do."

"Why? You found me irritating all the times before, and we had one conversation and I gave you a couple of orgasms and now suddenly I'm a good guy?"

"You also cook me bacon," she said, her voice small.

"You don't really know me."

And how did she tell him that she did? She knew the particular way the sun illuminated his hair and revealed wheat and gold and glory every time it did. How did she tell him that she knew the way that his eyes lit up when he saw a woman he wanted to take home, because she'd seen that happen more than once at a bar, and she had always been held captive by the dance between him and the woman that would never be her. How did she tell him that he had caused her pain on deep, deep levels? Shame. That he had made her question whether or not she was a good person. And yet she had still found a way to live her life and stay away from him, and some of that was because... She had admiration for him.

Some of it was because of him. Just like the other feelings were about him.

How did she tell him any of that?

She didn't even like going over it to herself. Because the more she sat with it, the more she dwelled on it—which she had never done when she was married—the more she had to acknowledge that he had been a thing always.

"I've seen you around. For a lot of years. I just think that you are a decent guy. If I didn't think that I would've handled all of this very differently. That's the truth of it. But I think that we can do this, and I think that we can be happy and... I just really want that."

She was begging him now. Pleading with him. "I really need to be happy."

"Then I'm going to do what I can to make you happy."

"Oh, don't get mixed up in that. You can't make me happy. But you can contribute to my happiness, or make things more difficult. I would like it if you were trying to contribute good things."

"What's the difference?"

"There's too many things that have happened to me that you didn't have anything to do with that have made things hard. So it can't be up to you to fix them."

"Yeah. Again, I don't see why."

"Because it isn't like that. Okay?"

He shrugged. And she had the feeling that wasn't an agreement. She had a feeling she hadn't one. She had a feeling that he was going to be a lot more difficult than she anticipated.

But if he would just shrug and make pancakes, then that was fine.

"Do you want to know the first time I thought you were beautiful?"

She lifted her face, her eyes clashing with his, horror hitting her square in the stomach. "I'm not sure that I do."

But part of her, this desperate, fluttering part of her, did want to know. Why wasn't that part of her dead? Why had not that part of her died with Chuck? This part of her that acted like a teenage girl, and wanted… To have her crush tell her that she was pretty. That's what he was. Her crush.

Her crush she was having a baby with. Her crush she'd slept with. But a crush nonetheless.

"Yeah. Well. Let's just get it out in the open. You

think that the way that we are is the way that it's going to be. So I think that we need to get some stuff out there. Don't you?"

"I don't know."

"Yeah. Well. I'm a decisive kind of guy. It's a risky proposition though it may be… I remember seeing you when you first got engaged to him. And you were hanging out down in front of the bar. I think you and your friends were angling to get some beers bought for you. But you were too young. And you were laughing. And I remember the way the sun kind of hit you from behind. And you were just lit up. And it wasn't just the sun. It was your joy. And I just remember your hair was so shiny and perfect, and your skin was brown all lit up in gold. And I wanted to touch you. And there was a ring shining on your finger, and I knew that I never would. And it's a funny thing. Because I have a level of deep acceptance about that which I can't change or have in this life. Which I'm not in charge of. That comes from loss. Maybe *acceptance* is a strong word, I don't know. But I get it. I'm not in charge of everything. But it just felt… It really felt like a kick in the face. In that moment. That I could want you like I did, but never have you."

The words took the breath out of her lungs, and like all other beautiful things in her life… They were a complication. She wanted to feel flattered, but that wasn't enough. It was too easy of a response. Too shallow.

"I didn't know," she whispered.

"Why should you? It wasn't a thing that could happen. It wasn't a thing."

Did she tell him? It felt risky. It felt like standing on the edge of a cliff. But if this really was about honesty... Could she actually let the unspoken hang between them? Or did she need to say something?

"The first time I noticed you I was in middle school. You were playing football. And I thought that you were... Like a movie star."

"Is that so?"

"Yeah. Unfortunately."

"So we just kept missing each other."

"Yeah. We just kept missing each other."

"Well, we managed to make it stick when we didn't miss, didn't we?"

"I am deeply uncomfortable with all of this," she said, putting her face in her hands.

"Life's uncomfortable."

"So are you... You're going to stay here? You're not going to go back out to the circuit?"

"Yeah. I expect that's what I'll do. I was looking for confirmation. On what I should do. And this pretty much decides it for me. I have something to stay for."

"Yeah."

And there was something about that that settled her. He had something to stay for. And she had something new to live for. This child.

And she was filled with terror about it all going away, but this felt good. It felt right.

They could do this. They could do this and it would be okay. It had to be.

"Shared custody." He was mumbling and muttering while he used a pickax to get granite up out of the ground to clear out the field, and finally, Jace acknowledged the muttering.

"What's going on?"

"She thinks that we're going to have a platonic relationship wherein we share custody of the child."

"Sounds mature," Jace said.

He looked at Jace. Hard. "And you would be fine with that?"

"I didn't say I would be *fine* with that. I said it sounded mature."

"Well. I'm not fine. And maybe I'm not mature."

"And what are you going to do about it?"

"I brought her breakfast this morning. And I aim to keep doing that."

"Keep bringing her breakfast?"

"Yeah. And dinner. I want her to see that she can't do this without me. Hell, I want to make it so she doesn't want to do this without me."

"And what do you want exactly?"

He thought of the way they'd been this morning,

sitting at the kitchen table, that low-level hum of need between them.

"I want her," he said. And suddenly, it was like the sky had broken open and rained down to hallelujah. Like God had slapped him across the face and said: finally, dumbass.

"I want her," he said again. Emphatically. "I don't want to be friends. I don't want to share custody. If we are going to have a baby, we need to be a family. And hell, how else am I supposed to keep her safe?"

"Fine. But what does that have to do with her?"

And he realized that was the thing. She had said that this needed to be about the baby. But for him it would never just be about the baby. He had wanted her, and they'd slept together because of that long-held desire between them. Longer than he'd ever even realized. At least on her end. And he couldn't separate the things. The pregnancy was a direct result of that desire. It wasn't on its own. It wasn't he could never be neutral about her. He never had been. He wanted her. In his bed every night and damn everything else. He wanted to keep her safe. And that meant keeping her with him. He wanted... He wanted to take care of her.

"Are you in love with her?"

Everything in him shied away from that. That felt like a bridge too far. That felt like the kind of wound you didn't come back from. And anyway, she might be attracted to him, but she was in love with a dead man.

"I want her. Functionally, for me, it's all the same."

"Well. Let's hope your plan to bait her with food works."

"I have some other things to fall back on if it doesn't."

"And that is?"

"She didn't get pregnant for just playing checkers."

"Yes. I guess not."

"How about you?" he asked. "You ever…"

He shot Kit a look. "Don't go there."

"I haven't gone anywhere. You don't even know what I was about to ask you."

"Was it about Cara?"

"Actually no. But way to go. You just shone a big ole spotlight on yourself."

"Well, no. Generically and to Cara, Cara needs to be protected at all costs. She's been through enough. She's a strong woman, and I care about her. But it isn't like that. Protecting her means… Never… Ever."

"What's so wrong with you?"

"I could ask you the same question, Kit."

"It's not about me," Kit said. "About love in general. It's a lot of work. I love you. I love everyone in this family. I'm going to have a kid. I… I don't need more. I don't need heavier. I know that Shelby feels the same way. Life has taken it out on her pretty hard too."

"Well, Godspeed. Make sure you include dessert with dinner."

"Good idea," he said.

He wasn't happy with any of this, but he had a plan. And that was the kind of man Kit was. If it was broken, he'd do his best to fix it. He may not have wanted to take on something like this, but he was now. And he would do the absolute best with it that anybody ever could.

Eleven

He went to her house every day for the next couple of weeks. He made breakfast, and three times a week, he made dinner.

They sat together and they ate it. And they talked about their childhoods—it was interesting to hear her side of the family dispute, which, of course, involved his ancestor cheating in a poker game and stealing the land from her family, and though he had already accepted that version of events after Chance and Juniper had gotten together, it was important that he heard it from Shelby herself—but they also found out they weren't all that different. They had been raised on the backs of horses. Raised to love this place. Generations of blood were soaked into the dirt. And they could respect that in each other.

He loved hearing about how her grandmother had taught her to be. How she'd learn to cook traditional recipes, and how her family tried to hang on to their traditions, their ways, as much as they could, while her parents also worked to give them all the advantages of the current culture right along with it. As someone who hadn't grown up with cultural tension, it was interesting to hear about it. And he found it meant something that she trusted him with the stories. They didn't talk about her marriage. They didn't talk about grief again. And they didn't really talk about the future.

But knowing about Shelby's foundation mattered.

He was supposed to be making her realize that she needed him. But all this was growing an attachment that he hadn't quite counted on. One that he hadn't anticipated.

But he had to wonder if Shelby just felt like they were growing that friendship she wanted. For him, it was something more. Something deeper.

He had her doctor appointment marked on his calendar, and when the day arrived, he got up early to make her breakfast like he always did, then he went to the bathroom and threw up. Though he didn't let her know about the throwing up.

He realized that he was… He was not handling this well. Because he knew as well as anyone that life just didn't always hand you good things. What if they went and there was no baby? What if all of this was gone before they got to have it? He wasn't sure that he could handle that. He wasn't sure... Yes. He wasn't sure about any of it. He knocked on the door, and she answered, looking tired. And maybe a little bit sick herself.

"You okay?"

"Yeah," she said. Then she groaned. "No. I'm nervous. Because if not for the positive pregnancy test, and the missed periods, I don't know that I would even know I was pregnant. And I did some online research..."

"Damnation, woman. Don't you know better than that?"

"It can indicate that you have a low level of hCG. Which could mean that something is wrong."

"Well, that's a fucked-up mess. Feeling worse when you're pregnant is better?"

"It's just what I read. I don't know... I don't know. I'm almost twelve weeks. So it's like... If everything is okay today, then maybe everything is okay. But what if it's not okay? What if we just spent all this time... For nothing?"

"Let me make you some breakfast."

"I don't think I can eat."

"Well, let's do our best."

He didn't tell her that he'd thrown his guts up forty-five minutes earlier. Because what was the point in letting her know that he wasn't any better off than she was? He wanted to spare her that. He didn't want to validate any of her worries.

He made a scaled-back breakfast, and they both did the best they could to eat. Maybe she was trying to be brave for him too. The thought made him smile a little bit.

"Let me drive," he said, opening up the passenger-side door of his truck and guiding her into it.

"Thank you," she said. "For being with me. It actually does mean a lot, and you know that I hate to admit that."

"I do know that, Shelby. I know you don't like to admit to needing anyone."

"I don't need you," she said, in defiance, and it made him laugh. In spite of it.

"Of course not," he said.

"I don't," she said. "I can't afford to need anybody. Not ever again. Needing people just… It just hurts in the end. It just hurts and hurts, and what's the point? You can't control whether or not you get to keep a person, so you can't really ever let yourself need someone."

"You know, I get that." Except he hadn't needed his sister. It wasn't that. But he understood how fragile everything was. "But I'm not sure that cutting yourself off from those kinds of connections is a good thing either."

"I didn't ask."

"I guess you didn't."

The little clinic that they went to just outside town was old and quaint and had definitely seen better days. And he didn't know what to expect from any of it. He'd never done anything like this before. Never been to a place like this.

"I come here for my yearly," she said. "So. You didn't need to know that." She was scribbling on paperwork and sitting deeply in one of the vinyl chairs.

"Why don't I need to know that?"

"It's not the kind of thing that we really need to share."

"I'm about to go into a doctor appointment with you. I can certainly handle mentions of your yearly."

And yet, it was notable in difference, because he had certainly never been in a relationship with a woman that was this intimate. And they'd only slept together one time. It was weird as hell.

But it also didn't feel... Bad. Not at all.

They got called into the room, and she sent him out while she got dressed in a hospital gown. He thought it was a little bit silly, all things considered. But when he came back in, she was lying on the table, covered by a blanket.

"So what exactly are they going to do?"

"I think they... Check for a heartbeat? And maybe do an ultrasound. To check how far along and all that."

"Well. We already know that," he said.

"True. I guess a lot of people can't be sure. But we're sure."

"Yeah. Pretty damn sure."

The door opened and an older, short man came in, and began to speak in a soothing voice, explaining exactly what he was going to do. Which was essentially what Shelby had said she thought would happen.

There was a small portable ultrasound machine and the doctor brought it up to the side of the bed. Kit suddenly felt frozen. He hadn't been prepared for this. He didn't know what the hell he'd been prepared for. But not this. Not the knowledge that they were going to see the child now. She looked similarly distressed, and reached out and took hold of his hand. He squeezed it tightly.

The doctor lifted up her gown and pushed the sheet low, before squirting a gel over Shelby's stomach, and putting the wand there. The sound was instantaneous. A strange pumping, whooshing sound that filled up the room. And then they saw movement. "Holy shit," he said, leaning into the screen. "Is that it?"

The doctor looked at him in a vaguely scolding manner, but Kit didn't care. "Yes. That's the baby." He wiggled the wand, and then moved it down lower. "And feet."

"And the heartbeat?" Kit asked.

The doctor moved the wand again, and he could see a fluttering gray thing, surrounded by black. "There it is. I'm just going to take some measurements."

Shelby squeezed his hand, and when he looked at her, he saw that her lips were pale. "Are you okay?"

She nodded, but didn't say anything.

"Based on what I'm seeing here, and on the dates you gave me... I'm going to put the date at March 1."

It seemed like both an eternity and a blink away. And he couldn't quite process the entire situation.

"Everything looks normal?" Shelby asked.

"Everything looks on track," the doctor said. "Exactly what I would expect to see."

"So I just... What do I do?"

"You come back in a month," the doctor said. "We should be able to do an ultrasound to establish the gender then if you'd like."

"Yeah," Shelby said, her eyes suddenly bright. "Okay."

The doctor left them, and Kit prepared to go too.

"It's okay," she said. "You can stay."

Without being asked, he turned to face the wall as she got up. He listened to the sound of her putting her clothes on. Fabric against skin.

Normally, he would be turning this into something a little bit more sensual. But for now... All he could think about was what he had just seen on the screen. All he could think about was the reality crashing in on him.

It looked so small and helpless. It was contained inside her body. There was nothing he could do. Nothing he could do to make sure that this went well. For him or for her.

"Are you okay?" he asked.

"Yeah," she said. "You can turn around now."

She was dressed again. And she looked so vulnerable. He wanted…

He wanted to protect her from everything. And what an uncomfortable feeling that was.

Because he knew that he couldn't. Because he knew that the world was cruel. Because he…

"Why don't we go home," he said. "You can take a rest. I'll be back by tonight for dinner."

And he realized that he'd said *home*, like it was theirs. But she didn't correct him, so he didn't bother to walk it back.

He didn't want to. And when he dropped her back at her house and said goodbye to her, he marveled at the fact that his relationships usually centered on sex. This one… Well, sex had certainly played a part in it, but there was all this other stuff, and it made it so singular. Different. Unlike anything he had ever even imagined.

In that sense, he was almost glad that she put a moratorium on the physical. Because it had forced them to get to know one another. It had forced them to build this other thing.

And he wanted to keep on building it.

He didn't know what that meant, or where it was headed.

But there was something about his plan that seemed unfocused now. It wasn't about him anymore. It was about her.

And that was the strangest realization of all.

Twelve

She woke up crying. She was glad she had the nap after the doctor appointment, but she had a dream… This dream where Kit was sitting in a rocking chair, shirtless, holding a tiny baby, somehow the epitome of her fantasies, both sexual and domestic all at once, and seeing him there with that familiar wood paneling behind him, seeing him enmeshed in her life, had made her cry in that dream. And when she'd woken up, the crying hadn't been only in the dream.

She tried to get herself together. She went to sit and work on a bracelet that she'd been beading for a few days now, but she couldn't focus.

She was pregnant. Really pregnant, and there was nothing wrong.

Kit had been there for her exhaustively... And she was... She was having a really hard time. With everything. She didn't understand how her life had gone from stagnant and stuck to this. She had wanted something different, but this was decidedly more different than she had been anticipating.

He was coming for dinner. He was cooking for her again. He did it for her all the time, and she just...

She was beginning to feel helpless. Like all these changes were spinning out of her control. It certainly wasn't the sweet, easier life that she had planned for.

That she had thought she would maybe begin to pursue.

Maybe the problem is you don't know what you want.

She did. She wanted the baby. She wanted everything to go smoothly with Kit.

She was not ready for him to show up, and when he did, she felt pretty raw still from everything.

"How are you?" And it was the concern that got her. The concern that made her want to run and hide from this. From him. But she didn't have the luxury of doing that. It was all supposed to be easy, right? Because they were friends?

Except when he breezed past her and went into her kitchen, grocery bags in hand, she had the sudden realization of why it wasn't easy.

They were having a marriage. All this intimacy, emotional and deep. Sex had at least been a distraction after their conversation about grief at the ranch, but... This was just all the emotional stuff. Nothing else.

He threw a dish towel over his broad shoulder and started to take ingredients out of the bag in front of him. She didn't know that was such a sexy thing to do, but it was. That sort of determined and focused competence. More than competence. The thing about Kit was that he was great at everything he did.

Get it together.

He got out a cutting board, and some vegetables, and began to slice through them with ruthless efficiency. And she was enthralled.

Trying to wrap her head around this moment. This life. And suddenly, it was like all the feelings were just too big for her. All of this. Because how was he here in her kitchen. And how was she here, pregnant with his baby? And what was her life? Was she still herself even?

It had seemed simpler when it was sex.

Because the sex wasn't like anything else. It was like a fantasy. It wasn't like her marriage. It wasn't like building a life. It was like burning everything to the ground. In an incendiary flame. It wasn't thinking or talking. It let her make him into something less complicated. Muscle and rough hands and a hard body.

That's what it let her have. And so she did what her body was begging her to do. What her senses demanded. She moved up behind him, and pressed her breasts to his back. She felt him go still. Completely and utterly still. He set the knife down flat on the counter, and then he growled, turning around and cupping her face, her chin held tightly in his palm. "What exactly are you offering me?"

And suddenly, this was dangerous Kit. The one who had put everything she knew in jeopardy every time she saw his face. The one who made her question everything.

It was that Kit. Yeah. That one.

"I would think that was pretty obvious," she said, sucking a sharp breath as she moved her hands to the front of his jeans. Her knees buckled. But thankfully, he was holding so tightly to her that she didn't fall. Because there he was. Hard and rigid already beneath her hand. Big and heavy and she could remember what it had been like to have him inside her.

Yeah. She could well remember.

Her breath hissed through her teeth as she let her fingers skim his hardened length. "I want you," she said.

"Do you?"

"Yes," she said. "I want you, now. In me."

"Me? Or are you thinking about someone else?"

"I have never thought about someone else when I wanted you."

And that was when he growled, feral and rough, and walked her back so that she was pressed flat against the kitchen wall. Her shirt was tugged up violently over her head, cast onto the floor. Her bra followed, and he kissed his way down her neck, her collarbone, took one of her sensitive nipples between his lips and sucked.

"Shit," he breathed. "You're more beautiful than I remembered."

He moved his hand with carnal reverence over her breasts, down her stomach, where he flicked open the button on her jeans and lowered the zipper.

Then he pushed his hand down beneath the waistband of her underwear, and found her wet with need for him. Because it only took a second.

She gasped, her head falling back against the wall as he began to stroke her. This was… This was that wild sex. That wild desire. Wild desire that she thought wasn't real.

It was so starkly different from what she'd had before. What she had before had been nice. What she had before had been manageable. And there was nothing manageable about Kit. He was too big. Too wild. Too much. He was something she couldn't control, and she'd been foolish just now thinking that she could. That this was her game. That she could take him and make him into something that she could dominate. It wasn't possible.

Because here in her house where she had built a life before, he was breaking her into small little pieces. Something she was afraid she would never be able to put back together. But her life was broken, so why shouldn't she be?

Is it broken, or are you just afraid of what's been built?

She shoved that thought aside, because she didn't want to think. She wanted pleasure. She wanted sex. She wanted Kit and his cock and nothing else. She didn't want anything more than this gloried, heady desire that was unlike anything she had ever experienced. And before she knew it, she was naked, with him fully clothed before her. He knelt down, lifted her leg up over his shoulder and parted her wide as his mouth made contact with the heart of her, already slick with her need as he began to lick her, deeper and deeper until she was shaking. Until she was clinging to his shoulders and crying out with unfulfilled desire.

Damn him. It was a blessing. A curse. Everything, all rolled into one.

It was light and shadow and impossibly out of reach.

And yet there she was, clinging to him for all she was worth, her fingers speared into his hair as she held his head right there. Just there. She rocked her hips, lost in the pagan rhythm that he set with his wicked tongue. And then she burst. Broke open. Shattered. Gasping and crying out his name.

And she knew that this was just another game that she had lost.

But before she could protest, he straightened, lifted her up, flipped that dish towel off his shoulder, set it on the counter and then set her bare ass right on top of that. "Didn't want you to be cold," he said against her mouth.

"Oh," she said, her brain a fog.

Then he stripped his shirt off and her mouth went dry. And her brain went blank.

He was the most beautiful man she'd ever seen.

And her need was a desperate thing. Clawing at her. And there was no biological excuse for it. She was already pregnant. She was already pregnant, and so there was nothing to hide behind. This was just need. Pure, filthy need. She'd already had an orgasm, but it wasn't enough. Because she wanted to feel his possession. She wanted his cock buried deep inside her. When she cried out his name.

She wanted him. All of him. She wanted to lose herself and find herself all at once. And she knew that the only way to do that was...

He undid the buckle on his jeans and tugged the zipper down roughly. She pushed his jeans down his lean hips, and he freed his arousal, drawing her close to him as he pressed slowly into her heat.

"Kit," she shouted, almost embarrassed by the intensity of the demand wound around his name.

She couldn't. She could not. And yet she was. They were. Because it was all the things and everything, and it was him and her together. Like nothing and no one had ever been.

Did everybody feel like this? Except, dimly, she knew that not everybody had this. So no. Not everybody felt like this. Because she'd never felt like this before. Like sex was a wonderful mystery that they alone had unlocked. That only they could ever figure the combination that would make this particular pleasure click.

He was so big and hard inside her, like he was made to fit her. Just a bit too much, but in the very best way.

She didn't want her sex comfortable. She didn't want it easy. She wanted hard and rough with a slight bite of pain. And he delivered. Cupping her ass as he pulled her against him, thrusting hard inside her and leaving her breathless each and every time.

His strokes were deep, and she lost herself in it. In this. In him.

She looked into his eyes, and she felt what burned there resonated in her soul.

And it terrified her. Made her tremble. Made her want to look away. Made her want to escape, but he held her face still as he drove into her again, and again. As her own desire wound around her like a golden thread, making her shiver.

Making her come apart at the seams.

And then she broke. Crying out his name just a moment before he shouted hers, spilling deep inside her, his hardness pulsing deep within her.

"Kit," she whispered. And he kissed her. Her mouth, her forehead, her cheeks. He kissed her and kissed her like there was nothing else he wanted to do in the whole world.

Like he was shocked and unmade by this thing she was.

In her house. In her little house that she had shared with Chuck for all those years.

And suddenly, she couldn't picture Chuck in it. And sadness closed her throat. Made her gasp. Made it hard to breathe.

"We'll have dinner later," he said, scooping her up and carrying her from the kitchen into the bathroom. As if he had been here a hundred times. As if he lived here. He turned the water on, and she waited, shivering as he undressed all the way. And when the water was warm, he put her in the shower and moved his hands over her body, gently, with great care. The warm water washed over her. And it did something to her. She didn't know if it was healing or hurting. She honestly couldn't tell.

"I..."

"Hey," he said. "You are okay. You're okay."

And she didn't know how he could say that. Because he didn't know. He didn't know. He wrapped his arms around her and pulled her naked body flush against his. He moved his hands over her curves, and he kissed her. Kissed her until she couldn't think.

Then he turned the shower off, dried her off and carried her to the bed, where he left her for a full forty-five minutes. And she just lay there. Feeling shell-shocked. Afraid that he would join her. Afraid that he wouldn't. And then he appeared wearing only a pair of jeans, holding two plates of food. He handed her one, and she took it, curled up beneath the blankets still. Then he got into the space beside her, on top of the blankets, his own plate on his lap. "How you doing?"

"Hungry," she said, drawing the plate up to her face.

"Good. Eat."

But how did she tell him? How did she explain the strange, fractured feeling blooming in her chest? Like a chip had been put into a windowpane long ago, and now the pressure, the cold, the heat, something, was making that crack expand. Spider outward.

"I think we should get married, don't you?"

And she didn't know how to say no. Not this time. Because what leg did she have to stand on? It had made sense to kiss him an hour ago. It had seemed like the best idea in the world. Like it would wrench some control back. Like finding that sexual connection again would somehow erase the tenderness that they'd found. But it hadn't. Here he was, in bed with her, eating dinner.

"I don't… I don't…"

"I want to take care of you," he said, and she was so grateful he'd said that. Because that wasn't marriage as she knew it. And somehow, that made it feel safer. "When my sister was sick, my brother and I made her a little wagon. And we decorated it. I spent hours taking her around in that thing. Like she was a little princess. And I loved it. I think I believed in things still. Different than I do now. Like I believed that there was some kind of healing power in love. I couldn't fix her. And if love could've healed her, then she would've been here. Believe me."

And oh, she knew that. She felt it. Deep in her soul, and it just hurt. It hurt so much to hear him say this, she wanted him to stop. It wrapped itself around her own grief and regret and pain. Around the futility of loss, and the merciless movement of the world as it kept on spinning even after your heart had been crushed.

She knew what it was like to wish love could save someone.

To be devastated that it couldn't.

Even as his words hurt, she felt closer to him. Felt like she understood him.

"And I'm… I spent a lot of years afraid," he said. "Afraid that I'd lose her. And then I did. And then I was afraid when my mom got pregnant with Callie. That something would happen to her. That something would happen to the baby. And it's like I've spent my whole life on this hypervigilant watch. Thinking that somehow… My love was gonna stop something from happening. My… My will for everything to be okay was going to fix something, and I always thought that caring was just so exhausting I never wanted to care for another person as long as I lived.

Not an extra one. But I care for you. I'll even give you a ride in a wagon if you want."

And her heart just felt like it cracked in two. Because she was tired. She was tired and he wanted to carry this. She was tired and he wanted to carry her. In a wagon. It wasn't some empty gesture from some guy who didn't know the weight of loss. He knew. And he still wanted this. And she could have it. Because it was different. Because… Because she was just so damned tired of being by herself. Because she wanted him to touch her every night. Because she wanted her baby to have a father. And maybe because she was scared and didn't want stigma.

"I'll marry you," she said. "I'll… Yeah."

"We don't have to have a wedding."

She nodded, tears filling her eyes. "Good. Good. I don't want to have another one."

"We just need to go sign the paperwork and do the thing. You don't even have to really formalize all that. We can have a court witness if you want."

"I would like that. Thank you. We can just tell everybody that we eloped. I think that would be for the best."

"Do you want me to move in with you or do you want to move in with me?"

And she realized she hadn't even been to his house. And she was torn. So torn, because having him here in this place, in her bed was… Unfathomable. But she had imagined raising the baby here.

"I don't know yet," she said.

"That's okay. We don't even have to move in together right away. We've got time."

"I hear a *but*."

"Yeah. But, I think we should get married. As quickly as possible."

"Are you afraid I'll change my mind?"

"Yes," he said. And she had to laugh. Because she sort of was too. And she couldn't really put her finger on why. No. She really couldn't.

"You want to go get a marriage license tomorrow?"

"Sure," she said.

"Do you want me to leave you alone tonight?"

She shoveled in the last bite of her dinner. "I don't know."

"I tell you what. I'm gonna stay."

And he stayed on top of the covers, with her naked beneath them, and pulled her to him, holding her close. And that was how they stayed all night.

Thirteen

Kit felt like he should feel a little more about getting Shelby to agree to marry him. Like he should feel triumphant or something. But he didn't. Instead, he felt a vague sense of disquiet that he couldn't quite put his finger on. Because he didn't feel… Like you did when you accomplished something. At least, not what he really wanted. But he couldn't quite figure out what he wanted. He couldn't really say either what had possessed him to tell her the story about Sophie. But nonetheless, the next day, they went to town with the appropriate documentation and went to the courthouse to file for a marriage license.

"Getting married again," the older woman in the

register's office said, smiling at Shelby. "I'm so happy for you, honey."

"Thank you," Shelby said, her cheeks going dark pink.

"We'll want to come back and do the thing in three days," Kit said.

"Not a problem," the woman said. "There are plenty of spots available. Just call ahead, and Sherm will be happy to do the ceremony."

"Great," he said.

"Boy, your families really did get rid of that feud, didn't they?"

"Yeah," Shelby said. "I guess you could say we did, Rose. Thank you."

When they walked back out of the courthouse, onto the main street of Lone Rock, which didn't hold a whole lot, Shelby looked tired. "I need to make a stop by Carefree Buffalo. They have some money for me. Because they sold a few of my pieces."

"Yeah," he said.

He walked down the street with her, and into a little shop that sold handmade knives, jewelry and leather goods.

There was a little corner with a variety of beaded items. Bracelets, earrings, barrettes.

"You did all these?" he asked, pointing to the display.

"Yeah," she said, looking embarrassed.

The owner of the store came out, and Shelby

greeted him, and what they were saying kind of faded into the background.

He watched her, and he watched her in a different way than he ever had. He knew her now. The rhythm of her. The way that she smiled, the way she laughed. The way she breathed. He had shared a bed with her last night, and he had never shared a bed with a woman all night. They hadn't had sex in that bed, and it had felt as astonishingly intimate as what had taken place in the kitchen. If not more so. He just... When she turned to look at him, a lingering smile from her conversation with the shopkeeper on her face, his heart stopped. Everything stopped. He was in love with her. He was in love with her, and that was why he wanted to marry her. He'd never been in love. He'd never wanted to be. He thought it sounded like work, and heavy work at that. But it didn't seem heavy, loving her. It was all in the showing up, every day. And it wasn't carrying the weight of the world on his shoulders. It was... Feeling like the weight of her and all her concerns wasn't all that heavy. And like maybe his life wouldn't matter if he was walking around carefree, with empty arms.

Maybe that was it. He just... He just wanted her. Her. And all of the baggage that came with it. And he didn't think she loved him. She loved Chuck. And that was fair. Maybe he was way too tied up in some things that made her feel guilty for her to ever have feelings for him. Or maybe she would just never be in love again. But that didn't change the way he felt. It didn't mean he didn't want her. Because he did. Dammit all, he did. But he knew he couldn't tell her. Not now. Because she just agreed to marry him, and he didn't want to rock that boat. So Kit Carson kept the truth of it to himself.

And it struck him, when he dropped her back off at her house, that he had probably loved her for a long time. And it had all just been about waiting for the right time. So he was still waiting for the right time. That was all.

Shelby didn't tell anyone in her family that she was getting married today. They had taken the first available spot with the judge that morning.

Kit had not spent the night. He hadn't the last two nights. They'd had dinner. They'd had sex. Because she couldn't keep her hands off him. And there was a wild determination in her need for him. But now that she'd given in to it, she didn't want to control herself at all. Was angry that she ever had. Now that she had given in, she wanted to do it over and over again. Because somehow it made... Somehow it made the fact that she was marrying him seem more distant.

But then he picked her up, and he was wearing a black button-down shirt, a black hat and a pair of dark jeans. And he was holding a beautiful bouquet of flowers, and suddenly everything seemed just a little bit too real.

"Hi," she said.

"You look beautiful."

But she'd worn jeans. And a tank top. And she suddenly felt like there was something wrong with her. But he said she was beautiful, and it made everything inside her hurt.

She didn't wear her wedding ring anymore. But suddenly the idea of wearing a different one...

But maybe he didn't have one. They hadn't talked about rings. But he had brought flowers.

They got into the truck, and he put it in Reverse. "Did you get rings?"

"I did," he said.

"Could we... Could we put them on now? Or after? But not during?"

"Whatever you need," he said.

"We can just put them on now," she said, starting to rummage through the bags that were in the truck.

And suddenly, he pulled over to the side of the dirt road they were still on, and took out the boxes with the rings. Then he took her left hand in his, and opened up the velvet box. Inside was the most stunning diamond she'd ever seen. "Kit..."

"I hope you like it. I got a carefree buffalo."

"It's beautiful."

His eyes met hers, there in the truck. And suddenly... Her stomach dropped. Because she thought that maybe if they put them on now it wouldn't feel the same. It wouldn't feel like marriage. It wouldn't feel like a promise. But as he slipped that band on her finger, she knew that she was an idiot. Because this felt so real. She had gotten a marriage license, and he was putting a ring on her finger, and it was real. "Shelby…" She went to pull away, but he put his hand on her cheek and held her fast, and then he was kissing her. Deep and hard.

"Kit…"

And then she couldn't speak, because it was them. Him. And she just always wanted him. No matter what.

And when they parted, he was breathing heavily. Then he opened up the next box. And inside it was a gold band. For him.

And she looked up at him, fear and regret coiling through her. "I can't."

And there was a grim sort of determined look on his face. "Well, I won't wear it until you can."

Then he steered the truck back onto the road, and they kept on going into town. It was a pretty short drive, and they got there and were able to park out front.

They went inside, and waited to be called into the judge's chambers.

"Good to see you," the judge said to Shelby.

"You too," she said.

Rose was their witness. And Shelby held the bouquet that Kit had brought in sweaty hands.

"None of your family come?" Rose asked.

"Well, I… No," Shelby said. "We didn't exactly tell them."

"You're eloping," said Rose. "So romantic."

Her hands trembled as Kit took them in his.

"We won't be exchanging rings," Kit said.

"All right," the judge said, clearly not put off by it at all. But she imagined that in the world of courthouse weddings, that wasn't all that uncommon. But then it came to vows. And she could feel tears pushing against her eyes. Feel herself breathing far too hard. "Do you, Shelby Sohappy, take this man to be your lawfully wedded husband? In sickness and in health, for richer or poorer, as long as you both shall live?"

As long as they lived. That was it. As long as you lived. That was all.

It ended after that. Her first marriage had ended. And here she was, on the verge of another life.

She was terrified.

"I do," she said before she could lose her nerve.

"And do you, Kittredge Carson, take this woman to be your lawfully wedded wife? To have and to hold, in sickness and in health, as long as you both shall live?"

And it was like the world stopped. The whole world. "I do," said Kit.

"And now, by the authority given to me by the state of Oregon, I pronounce you husband and wife."

And without being told that they could kiss, Kit pulled her into his arms, and kissed her. And she clung to him, kissing him back, because he was the lifeline in the moment, even as he was the thing that made her tremble.

And when they parted, it was over. She had a husband. Another husband. But Kit wasn't another of anything. He was… Somehow she had married Kit Carson.

And she didn't know how she was ever going to get her head around that. She expected him to drive her back home. But he didn't.

"Kit…"

"I decided we ought to have a honeymoon."

"A honeymoon?"

"Yeah. Just…figured we'd stay at a nice place on the Deschutes River. Enjoy the view. Some good food."

And she found that she didn't have words. She didn't even know what to think. He turned on the radio, and there was a Jimmie Allen song on, and she tried to focus on the lyrics, and not on her confusion as they drove on the highway, headed north.

"Where exactly are we going?"

"Bend," he said.

"Oh. I didn't know you were wanting to go into the city."

He chuckled. "I just thought it might be nice to go somewhere a little… You know. Nice."

It took two hours to get there. They pulled into a hotel that she'd never been to before. Right there on the Deschutes River.

"I packed an overnight bag for us," he said as he reached into the back of the truck and produced it, before getting out and heading into the lobby.

And she just sat there. Feeling stupid.

Then she got it together, unbuckling and scrambling out behind him, walking into what was a beautiful, woodsy room with high ceilings and metal art all over the place. Fish and elk wrought from iron standing proud over stone tiles.

"This is beautiful," she said.

"I just wanted... I wanted something to mark the day."

And suddenly, she just wanted him. She wanted him, because it might do something to blot out the feelings that were rioting through her. The things that felt sharp and jagged and a little bit broken.

It took a moment for them to get all checked in, and then they went upstairs, to the suite down at the end of the hall.

"Kit," she breathed. "This is too much."

And she hadn't fully appreciated until just then that she had married a man with money. She just hadn't thought about it at all. Well. That was... Handy. She supposed. Except she didn't really want for much of anything in her life. Except she...

And then she couldn't think, because Kit was kissing her.

And at least when Kit was kissing her, she could blot out all her doubts and just feel.

Fourteen

He kissed her like he was starving, because he was. Like he was gasping for air and she was the only source.

He should've told her his plans. He could see that she was a little bit shell-shocked. The rings, the vows, everything, that it had all been a little bit much for her. And it was tearing him apart. Breaking him open. Because he needed her. He needed this. He wanted… He wanted her to feel like his wife. Because she damn well felt like it to him. He wanted this to matter. He wanted it to be everything.

Maybe he wanted too much.

But life had knocked him down and kneed him in the groin enough times for him to know that things weren't magic. For him to know that this might be hard. For him to know that he might always be competing with a love that had been thwarted before its time had come to an end. And maybe there was no competing with that. Not ever. But he didn't want to compete anyway. Not really. He wanted to be different. He wanted to be singular. He wanted to be new. He wanted to be Shelby and Kit, nothing that had come before. And nothing that could ever come after. He wanted to be everything.

And so he kissed her, walking her back to the bed as he stripped the tank top, the jeans, the determined nonwedding outfit from her body. Whatever she needed to do. But he wanted her to be his.

If this was the only way to do it, if this was the only way to reach her, then he damn well would. So he stripped her naked, the sight of her bronze curves filling him with awe, filling him with need. He wanted this woman. He wanted her more than he wanted his next breath.

"Lie down," he ordered. "I want to look at you."

"Kit..."

"You're my wife," he said. "You're mine."

And suddenly, a deep feeling of possession burst inside him. He could scarcely breathe around it. Couldn't think. All he could do was feel.

"Damn, you're so pretty. So damned pretty."

The words came out rough, almost violent. But it was a violence in him. Tearing through him, rioting through his chest, making him feel like a stranger to himself.

And there was a glint of something, something like fear in her dark eyes, and he wanted to make it go away. But he also wanted to push. To push past it.

Because every time they came to this point, and it felt like an important thing, they didn't get further. Something stopped them. There was a barrier that went up, and he didn't know what that was. Didn't know how to fight it. And he wanted to. Because he wanted... He wanted everything.

He stood at the foot of the bed and began to take his clothes off slowly.

He looked at her, and he knew that she wanted him. He knew that she wanted this, this thing that burned between them hotter and brighter than anything.

He slowly undid the buckle on his jeans, undressed and moved to the edge of the bed. "Get on your knees," he commanded. She obeyed, and it was a strange and beautiful thing to see her, still filled with fire, but not fighting against him at all.

"Take me in your mouth, Shelby."

And he made sure to keep his gaze locked with hers, to hold her captive with his eyes as she moved forward, curling her fingers around his aching cock as she lowered her head to take him into her mouth.

The soft sound she made vibrated through his body, and he thought his soul had exited the building.

Kit was pretty sure he was deceased. A ghost. Just from that soft, slick contact from her lips. Her tongue. She lowered her head and took him in deep, pulling back slightly when it was clear it was a little too much for her. And there was something about it that thrilled him. Something about it that made him feel like a god. And maybe that was wrong. Maybe it was messed up. But he didn't care. Because… How could it be? How could it be when he just loved her? When he wanted to possess her in every way. That was the thing. When he wanted all of it, every last thing. Her and nothing more. And he wanted… He wanted her to prove to him right now, beyond a shadow of a doubt, that it was more than just desire. Because while it was desire on a level he had never known, it was something more.

She'd been under his skin for a long damned time. And he knew what it was now. That thing that he was so afraid of. That thing he could never name. And why would he? She'd been off-limits to him. In love with someone else. And it was entirely possible she still was. Entirely possible that he was competing against her love for a dead man. And he was alive. So he would make mistakes. He would frustrate her. They were going to have a child together. They were going to be under different stress. And she hadn't chosen him. Maybe it would be easy for her to resent him. Maybe he would never be able to live up to all that. But they had this. They had this, and she was sucking him like he was her favorite damn thing. And that was real.

Maybe for her it wasn't love. But he would take emphatic, absolute need. He would take desire that was undeniable. Desire that transcended common sense. Desire that was more, shot higher, farther into the stratosphere than anything else either of them had ever experienced. And for him, it would be love. Always.

And it was like some truths broke open inside him. All around him. All that stress, all that care. It was love. Always. And the grief that he felt over the loss of his sister was all that love with no one left to care for. But it was still there. Love was something that couldn't be taken away. And somehow, during a blow job, he was having the single greatest moment of clarity in his life. Maybe because he had never loved anyone or anything more than Shelby. Maybe because he loved the vision of the life they could have. Enough to risk everything. But even if that vision didn't come out perfect. Even if it was never everything, he would love her. Because love was a sacred space, one he could choose to dedicate his whole soul to. One that could live on, no matter what was given in return. No matter what.

He felt himself reaching the end of his control, and he gripped her hair tight, guiding her head back up. "I want to be inside you."

Her lips curved up into a coy smile. "I mean. Technically you were."

"You know what I mean."

"Yeah," she said, but the word was heavy, and it was like she knew. Heavy with need. Heavy with the intensity of all that they were. And he was on fire with it.

On fire with all of it.

He kissed her. Drowning in her. If he never had anything but her, it would be okay. He wasn't marrying her for the baby. He'd married her for her. And she was his wife.

His wife.

His knees nearly buckled with the wonder of it. He kissed her, laying her flat on the bed, her legs parting for him. And he entered her in one smooth thrust. The feeling of her body holding him like this, of being in her, overwhelmed him, no matter how many times it happened.

He knew she'd only had one lover other than him. And he had a fair few. But none of it mattered. Not now. Because this wasn't like anything. She wasn't like anything. They were altogether new and glorious. They were the stars.

He could remember well that night, before the first time he'd ever touched her, when he looked up at the sky and noticed those stars.

Like he was seeing them for the first time. She made him see things. She made him feel things. She took him from the gray haze of grief, and she painted his world all different colors.

And he never wanted to go back. And he didn't have to. He lost himself in her. Over and over again. And when she trembled beneath him, crying out his name, he released hold on all of his control. All of it. He kissed her, his mouth against hers as he said the only thing that existed inside him. The only truth. The only thing that mattered. "I love you."

She was lying there, awash in sensation and pleasure after the intensity of their coming together, and his words were rolling over her like a tsunami. And she couldn't find anything to grab on to. She didn't know what to do. She was drowning. In sorrow, and guilt. And regret. He loved her? He loved her.

That wasn't possible. Not Kit Carson. Kit Carson, that object of her desire. Whom she had considered dangerous and something else altogether. Because he had been part of the Carson family.

Because she was supposed to love someone else. She did love someone else. She did.

She did.

And she couldn't betray him. Not like this. Not like that. When she had… She had wanted Kit. She had wanted Kit while she was married, and if she loved him now too, and she was having a baby with him, then what had she kept for the man she'd made vows to?

You made vows to Kit too.

She couldn't breathe. She was panicking.

"You don't need to say anything," he said. "But I wanted you to know. I didn't marry you because of the baby. I married you because I wanted to be your husband. Because I fell in love with you, Shelby. I don't know when. It seems silly to say years ago, but maybe it was then. But for sure in these last weeks. It was like all that electricity between us came together and started to make sense. Maybe it was just waiting for the right time. Hell, I don't know. But I love you. I love talking to you. I love being with you. I love being in you. And I don't ever want to be with anyone else. Not ever again. I just… I just love you. And when I say that, it's from a position of having worked really hard to climb that mountain. But I realized something. I love my sister, even though she's gone. But I love her still. I don't know. I guess I felt like I lost that. But I didn't. I still get to have it. I still get to have love. It's a miracle."

He was being so raw. So honest.

It was Kit and she couldn't handle it.

It was so deep and she didn't want to go that far. She couldn't.

"I don't feel that way," she said. "Because it isn't the same. I had a husband. And I loved him."

She felt sick. She felt like she was going to throw up. Or maybe die.

"I had a husband and I loved him. And I can't…"

"What?"

"I just feel so guilty. I feel like I'm betraying him. And myself. I feel like... I don't want this. I don't want to love you. I can't love you."

"Shelby. I'll wait. I don't need you to do a damn thing. We can go on like we have. Like we always have. We can go on like this."

"Maybe you can," she said. "But I can't. I just don't think I can. I think... I think it was a mistake."

"It wasn't a mistake."

"All of it was," she said. "How can I... How can I think that this would work? I just... It isn't going to. It can't."

"Shelby, my love isn't dependent on you giving it back. All I know is that the first time I noticed you, it changed something for me. And it took all these years for it to lead here. I can wait more years. I can wait more."

And she didn't know why that infuriated her. Why he was acting like this was okay. Like maybe it was a good thing. When that word, when the idea of him...

"This isn't love. Not as I understand it. This... This is something else. It's chemistry. It's desire. I want you. I want to be with you. I like you to do things to me that I've never liked before. I like doing things to you that I've never liked before. I always knew I wanted your body, Kit. But that's the kind of man you are. You're a really great body."

Guilt lashed at her.

"Is that all?"

"It's all you can be for me."

"Well, I'm the body that married you. I'm the body that helped to make this baby. I'm the body that loves you. But I'm gonna prove to you that there's not a time frame on this. I want you to take my truck, and go home. Take all the time you need."

"This is our honeymoon."

"You just said you didn't want all that."

She felt like her pain was pushing her into the ground. Like she was being driven farther and farther into a hole.

"I just want to leave you with one thing."

"What's that?"

He turned around and took something out of his overnight bag. The box that had his ring in it.

"Now what I want you to do is keep this. And when you're ready, you put it on my finger."

"I won't… I can't…"

"Then you give it back to me."

She couldn't, though. She couldn't make her hand release it. She wanted to be able to have him in her life. She wanted to keep sleeping with him. She wanted him to be a father to her child. She wanted… She wanted all of that without any risk. And it was a misery. Standing there frozen. Not being able to take either thing that she wanted. Not being able to be… As strong as she wanted to be. As good as she wanted to be. As brave.

"That's what I thought. Hang on to it."

"How are you going to get home?" she said.

"Don't worry about me, Shelby. I'll figure it out. I've got family. I've got time."

She took the truck keys, and she took the ring. And she started to collect her clothes. Then she walked out of her honeymoon suite like she hadn't just entered an hour before. She walked out with her heart on the ground, or maybe it was just back in the room with him. All she knew was that she needed to protect something. Except right now… She felt like she didn't have anything.

You have his truck keys, and his wedding ring.

Yeah. She had those two things. And what the hell was she supposed to do with them?

Fifteen

Well. That had not gone well. He sat down, bare-ass naked on the end of the bed in his honeymoon suite. And he did something he really didn't want to do. He called his brother.

"Hey, Chance," he said. "You up for driving to Bend?"

"When?"

"You know. Now, maybe?"

"Why?"

"Well, I'm in Bend. Because I got married and my wife just left me and took my truck."

"What the fuck did you do?" asked Chance.

"I didn't do anything, actually. But thank you. I just told her that I loved her."

"Oh. Well. I'll be there in a minute."

It didn't feel like a minute. And really, it wasn't. It was a hell of a long time before his brother managed to get there, and by the time he did, Kit was a little bit drunk.

"Oh, boy," said Chance. "So she rejected your ass?"

"Yeah. I... I'm in love with her, Chance. I'm in love with her... And... She's not in love with me."

"I think that's bullshit. I think you know that too."

"Do I?"

"Yeah. I think so. I think she's scared."

"Yeah. I get that."

"And why exactly aren't you scared anymore?" Chance asked.

"I don't know. The same reason you aren't. Love is just more important."

"It is."

"I'll wait for her."

"That's how you know it's real. It feels urgent. But if you can be patient... If you could be patient, then... It's the real thing."

"I've been patient."

"Yeah, I know."

"It's all right with me if she still loves him. Maybe for her, that's how it will always be. But for me... It's fate. There's nobody else but her."

"I don't see why you can't be her fate too."

"Well, I respect what she had."

"You're here. And you're together. I suspect that

her real problem is that she's a little bit afraid that you and her might have been inevitable."

Well. That made sense. But it was a damned optimistic view.

"And how is it that you have so much faith in that?"

"Because it took amnesia, a very strange lie and a whole lot of letting go for me to find love, but I did it anyway. I believe you'll have the same. So… That's it. I just believe in it."

He was going to cling to that. And he did. The whole ride back to Lone Rock. That was what he clung to.

Sixteen

She should go talk to Juniper. She should go talk to somebody. Anybody. But instead she found herself driving to the graveyard. It made her feel grim and sad, and she didn't go there all that often, because there was something so definitive about it that she just hated.

But that plot had been meant for the both of them. And there was just something... There was just something... She parked in the cemetery parking lot and lowered her head over the steering wheel and started to cry. Deep, wrenching sobs. And somehow, she couldn't make herself get out.

Finally, she did. Finally, she caught her breath enough to do that.

She got out of the truck and walked down the familiar path to where Chuck's gravestone was.

"This is weird," she said. "I'm not given to talking to you. I guess you know that. Or you don't. I... I don't know how I feel about it."

But the stone was unresponsive. And the ring was heavy in her pocket.

Real.

The weight of it was real.

Present.

Here.

Now.

And suddenly, she felt so stark and clear what Juniper had said to her when she'd first confessed that she was pregnant, and the guilt that she felt. That Chuck would never be a father, that he would never have had that dream, but she was moving on and living. Because she was alive.

She didn't know if she believed in the idea that a person had a set number of days. In the idea that when it was your time it was your time. In fact, she had resisted that hard, because it had felt like in no way could it be her twenty-six-year-old husband's time.

But she supposed in the end it didn't matter. He had the years and the life he'd been given. And they'd been happy.

Her heart had been his, because she'd given it to him, and even with her attraction to Kit, she had devoted her love and her body to the man she'd made her vows to.

Till death do us part.

And it had parted them. So much earlier than she'd anticipated. But it had.

And she was holding herself back. Holding herself back with a foot in her old life. No. Worse. With her heart in her old life.

What if she let go? What if she listened to Kit?

Listened to what he'd said. That love wouldn't go away. It wasn't gone. It was different. But it lived in her. What if she trusted that? And what if she quit feeling so damned guilty that she had fantasies about Kit?

She wanted to cry. Wanted to weep at the injustice of everything.

But not at the life she was living now. For the first time in a very long time. She was angry that the world was cruel and Chuck had died too young. But she wasn't angry that she was here with Kit. She wasn't angry that she was having his baby.

"I'm happy."

And she had to put her hand over her mouth to stifle a sob.

She was happy. She loved Kit.

And the sound that tore from her body was half exultation, half despair.

She loved Kit Carson. And it wasn't like anything else. They were everything. They were obsession and heat and fire and love. They were a previously undiscovered passion that she hadn't known existed. They were connected. And they always had been. And if fate was real, then maybe she had to accept that she'd been walking toward him all this time.

Maybe she had to accept that she had been Chuck's fate. And they'd had love. And it had been real. But where his road ended, hers kept going. He had been love. And it had been real. But her fate went on. It went forward.

She felt...giddy and guilty and afraid, because how could it be this easy? How could it be this clear? Was it okay that Kit felt like fate? Was it okay if he might be the love of her life?

And on the heels of that came desperation. Fear. And it all became clear. It wasn't the guilt. It was that what she felt for Kit was so big... That if she loved again, and she lost again... She had survived Chuck. But she couldn't survive losing Kit.

She couldn't survive it.

She loved him. In a deep, all-consuming way. As a woman who had known loss. As a woman who had known risk. As a woman who had been married before, and knew what things she would do differently now. Yeah. Because she knew a good marriage. But she also just knew marriage. And the truth was, if she could start from scratch... Kit would be whom she chose. Because they had something more complete. They had a chemistry that you couldn't deny.

And that didn't mean she regretted what she had before. She didn't. It didn't mean it didn't matter. But she was older, and had more perspective. And she knew… She knew the hardship that life could bring your way. She knew the cost of love.

But oh, admitting that Kit was more… That was… She felt like her soul had been bruised. There was the pain of what was behind her, and the fear of what was before her, and she just… She didn't know quite how she was going to go on. Except she could. Because she was here. And it was a gift.

And she remembered the wonder on Kit's face when he'd said that he loved her. When he'd shared with her his realization about love.

There was still more to learn. For him. For her. They were having a baby. And they were married.

She knew why she was here. She had to leave the idea of no one but Chuck as her husband behind her. She had to put away the visions of the life she thought she would have. Because when she put Kit's ring on his finger, he was the one and only. He was the love of her life. Because her life stretched out before her. Her fate, because how could he be anything else?

"You were a good husband," she said. "And I loved our life. It ended too soon. And now I have to keep living. Now I get to keep living." And it was like a weight had been lifted from her shoulders. This revelation that made her feel bruised also made her lit up.

Because she could be happy. There was no limit to that happiness. There was no limit to the love. If only she was willing to stop standing in the past. She had already experienced the loss. And no amount of clinging to it would change it.

No amount of clinging to it would keep her safe.

It would just keep her living a half life, and she needed to want better for herself. She really and truly did.

She walked back to the car, tears still on her cheeks. And she took her phone out of her pocket and dialed her sister. "Juniper... Do you by any chance know where Kit is?"

"As a matter fact I do. But... After you find him... You and I need to talk. Just about everything that's happened."

"Yeah. We do. But after I find Kit."

Kit was sitting at his house, on the front porch. And he knew that waiting out here today was probably pretty foolish. But... He couldn't bring himself to stop waiting. Couldn't bring himself to stop looking.

And then, his own truck came driving up the road. It was his wife.

His heart leaped up into his throat.

She parked in front of the porch, and got out, scrambling toward him, and his initial response was to feel worried. Seeing those tears on her face.

"Are you okay?"

She started to cry. Deep, wrenching sobs that shook her shoulders. "How can you ask that? After what I did to you. How can you still care?" she sobbed. "How can that be the first thing that you ask?"

"Because I love you. Because I've decided to care no matter what."

"I'm okay," she said. "I'm just... I love you," she said.

And he knew they needed to talk. He knew they did. But right now all he wanted to do was kiss her. Kiss those words right from her lips. "I love you," he growled, and he carried her up the steps into the house. They were a fever. She tore his clothes from his body, and he tore hers from hers. This was theirs. It had been theirs for all these years, and they hadn't been able to do anything about it, and now they could do whatever they wanted.

So he stripped her bare, and laid her down on the floor, made her cry out her love for him at least ten more times before he satisfied them both, shaking as he found his pleasure inside her.

"I love you."

And then he picked her up, ready to carry her to the bed.

"Wait," she said.

"What?"

"I just have to get..." She scrambled down from his arms, and grabbed her pants, then she took the ring box out of the pocket.

"I have this for you."

"Damn, sweetie."

They were naked, in his living room, and she was standing in front of him like she had at their wedding.

"I just wanted… I just needed… I want to make vows just for you. For us. Vows that are like the stars we looked at together. Because I thought a lot about what I want. I thought a lot about marriage. About what it is. And about what I want us to have." She brushed a tear away from her face. And he knew right then that no bride could ever have been more beautiful than his. Naked in front of him. Honest and open and not hiding at all.

"Kit Carson," she said, "I think you might be my fate." He'd never cared much for that word. Because he hadn't had a lot of good things in life that could be attributed to fate. But he wanted to believe she was fate. That they were.

So he chose to believe it.

She drew in a jagged breath. "And I have spent a long time trying to avoid that thought. I felt guilty that I was attracted to you. It felt like a sin. And I wanted to make it something less than it was. But my road was always going to lead to you, whether I knew it or not. I can tell you honestly that I made vows to another man, and I kept them. But he's not my husband anymore. I just say that, because I want you to know that these vows that I'm making to you I'm going to keep. I'm gonna keep them with everything I am."

A tear trailed down her cheek and he reached up and wiped it away. He wanted to make all of her pain easier. Always. He knew too much about life to think he could keep her from it entirely, but he could carry some of it.

"I'm not married to you because of the baby," she said. "I know that marriage is more than that. Deeper than that. I love you, and I want to share a life with you. House with you. A bed with you. I love you because you make me feel things I didn't know were possible. I love you, because... Even just talking to you... It made me feel like I could shake myself out of this hole that I was standing in. That place where I was stuck. You made me feel that way. And I really wanted that. But then we... We became more. We became what I think we were meant to be."

"Shelby... I love you. And I know for a fact that I was meant to be with you. And there were all these things, all these terrible things that made me feel like I couldn't be with anyone, but when I sat back, and I honored what I lost instead of just being angry about it... That was when it made sense. That was when I could love you. And I really do love you."

"I love you too," she said. "So much. I love you so much and it was all just fear. I'm not gonna say I don't... That I don't feel any now. I do. It's scary. Feeling all of this. It's terrifying. Because, Kit... You're everything in a way no one else has ever been. The way that we talk. The way that we are. And I resisted… The image of you in my house, the image of you in my life, because… It's just so much. It's everything. I was never afraid that I couldn't care about you enough. I was always afraid that if I admitted it, it would be too much. And I promise you… If it ever feels like too much, I'm not going to pull away again. I'm going to lean right in."

And then she took the ring out of the box, and took his hand in hers. And she slipped that band onto his finger. "For better or worse. In sickness and in health. Till forever."

"Till forever," he agreed.

"Also…six inches is patently not enough."

He chuckled. "Glad you came around to seeing things that way.

"I love you,"

"It was always you," she said. "It's always you."

Epilogue

Their daughter might not be able to walk yet, but she made a beautiful flower girl.

And when Shelby Carson married her husband for the second time, with a wedding dress and both families in attendance, and no tiara, it was one of the happiest days of her life. She had wanted to have a wedding, a real one, because she wanted everybody to share this with them. But the happiest day of her life was the day she had chosen him for real. For always.

She looked at the head of the aisle, and she saw him standing there. Her gaze had always found him. Always, for all these years.

And she knew that it always would.

* * * * *

#2905 THE OUTLAW'S CLAIM
Westmoreland Legacy: The Outlaws • by Brenda Jackson
Rancher Maverick Outlaw and Sapphire Bordella are friends with occasional benefits. But when Phire must marry at her father's urging, their relationship ends...until they learn she's carrying Maverick's baby. Now he'll stop at nothing to stake his claim...

#2906 CINDERELLA MASQUERADE
Texas Cattleman's Club: Ranchers and Rivals • by LaQuette
Ready to break out of her shell, Dr. Zanai James agrees to go all out for the town's masquerade ball and meets handsome rancher Jayden Lattimore. Their attraction is instantaneous, but can their connection survive meddling families bent on keeping them apart?

#2907 MARRIED BY MIDNIGHT
Dynasties: Tech Tycoons • by Shannon McKenna
Ronnie Moss is in trouble. The brilliant television host needs a last-minute husband to fulfill her family's marriage mandate before she turns thirty—at midnight. Then comes sexy stranger Wes Brody, who volunteers himself. But is this convenient arrangement too good to be true?

#2908 SNOWED IN SECRETS
Angel's Share • by Jules Bennett
After distillery owner Sara Hawthorne and Ian Ford spend one hot night together, they don't expect to see each other again...until he shows up for their scheduled interview about her family business. Now snowed in, can they keep it professional?

#2909 WHAT HAPPENS AFTER HOURS
404 Sound • by Kianna Alexander
Recording studio exec Miles Woodson needs a showstopping act for his charity talent show, and R & B superstar Cambria Harding fits the bill. But when long days working together become steamy nights, can these opposites make both their passion project and relationship work?

#2910 BAD BOY WITH BENEFITS
The Kane Heirs • by Cynthia St. Aubin
Sent to audit his distillery, Marlowe Kane should keep her distance from bad boy owner Law Renaud. But when a storm prevents her from getting home, they can't resist, and their relationship awakens a passion in both that could cost them everything...

Returning to her hometown, brokenhearted journalist Adaline Harlow is supposed to write an exposé on Colter Ward, Texas's Sexiest Bachelor, and that assignment does not include falling for him! As the attraction grows, will they break their no-love-allowed rule for a second chance at happiness?

Read on for a sneak peek at
Most Eligible Cowboy
by USA TODAY *bestselling author Stacey Kennedy.*

"You want your story. I want these women off my back… Stay in town and agree to being my girlfriend until this story dies down and I'll give you the exclusive you want."

"Her eyes widened. "You're serious?"

"Deadly serious," he confirmed. "I want my life back. You need a promotion. This is a win-win for both of us."

She gave a cute wiggle on her stool. "I think you're giving me far too much credit. Why would women care if I'm your girlfriend?"

"I don't think you're giving yourself enough credit." He stared at her parted lips, shining eyes, her slowly building smile, and closed the distance between them, waiting for her to back away. When she didn't and even leaned in closer, he said, "Trust me, they'd care." He captured her mouth, cupping her warm face, telling himself the whole damn time this was a terrible idea.

Don't miss what happens next in...
Most Eligible Cowboy
by USA TODAY *bestselling author Stacey Kennedy.*

Available November 2022 wherever
Harlequin Desire books and ebooks are sold.

Harlequin.com